Cakewalk to Murder

The Painted Lady Inn Mysteries

By

MK Scott

Books by M K Scott

The Talking Dog Detective Agency
Cozy Mystery
A Bark in the Night
Requiem for a Rescue Dog Queen
Bark Twice for Danger
The Ghostly Howl
Dog Park Romeo

The Painted Lady Inn Mysteries Series
Culinary Cozy Mystery
Murder Mansion
Drop Dead Handsome
Killer Review
Christmas Calamity
Death Pledges a Sorority
Caribbean Catastrophe
Weddings Can be Murder
The Skeleton Wore Diamonds
Death of a Honeymoon
Cakewalk to Murder

The Way Over the Hill Gang Series
Cozy Mystery
Late for Dinner
Late for Bingo
Late for Shuffleboard (June 2019)

Chapter One

THE JUDGES STROLLED to the next baker standing proudly by a five-layer cake dusted with cocoa and decorated with live violets.

"This is the one," Donna declared and scooted up in her wing chair to be even closer to the television.

Her college-aged helper, Tennyson, who she often referred to as Ten, stroked his scruffy beard. It was a fair imitation of her husband, Mark, in his contemplation mode. Ten dropped his hand and shook his head. "I don't know. What about Alastair? He used all those egg whites to make his cake lighter."

"Please." She lengthened the word, then gave a derisive snort. "That's so old-fashioned. My great-grandmother did it. Judges want something new and cutting edge, while still bringing indescribable joy to their taste buds."

"You think putting flowers on a cake will do it?"

A door sounded in the distance before Donna could reply. Currently, there were no guests in the inn, and she had locked all the doors, guaranteeing she could have peace while watching "The Great British Bake Off" show. Unfortunately, she couldn't lock out Tennyson, who had taken an interest in the program.

Jasper, her aging puggle, gave a welcome bark. It meant Mark was back from his Chamber of Commerce meeting, which he agreed to attend so Donna could watch the show in real time. If she had recorded it, Janice would ruin it by calling her up, telling who the winner was, and would make all manner of comments as if she had actually seen the show. No, thank you.

The judges talked amongst themselves as the tension built. Often, she imagined herself on the show and what she would make to tempt the finicky judges. The contestants must be nervous. Strangely enough, Donna was, too. A throw pillow found its way into her hands, and she squeezed it as the judges mentioned the third and second place finishers. They might have called them winners, but almost everyone conceded there was only one winner.

"And the winner is…" The lead judge paused for a moment. "Alastair! With his lighter than air angel food cake. It reminded me of my dear old Granny and her ability to make every moment special."

Disgusted, Donna tossed the pillow in the direction of the television. It fell short by a few inches. "I can't believe it!"

This was so wrong. Tennyson laughing his fool head off didn't help, either. She turned to tell him so and discovered her husband standing in the entrance with a secretive smile. What was up with that? The half-dozen Chamber meetings she attended didn't make her smile. Whenever there was more than one person on a committee, there would be endless arguments. Last time, the florist suggested they needed town colors. That took ninety minutes of her life that she would never get back.

Mark knew how to work a room, and he waited a full minute until he had their attention. "I bet I know something else you won't believe."

He did deadpan so well that it was hard to tell if her husband was teasing or not. "Gary Manson, the owner of the music store, thinks Legacy should have its own song?"

"Yes. He's working on it, too, but that's not it. It's something else. Something you might like. In fact, I know you'll love it!"

Her husband could be thoughtful, especially when it came to creative gifts. This one might be the best. She pushed up out of her chair and hugged Mark tight. "You're the best husband in the world!"

"I haven't even told you yet."

"No need. I know."

"How could you?"

Her euphoria dimmed a little as she got a tiny twinge that possibly she and her husband were not on the same page. "You were going to tell me you were going to attend all future chamber of commerce meetings without me? You're so much better at that kind of thing, and they love seeing you there."

"No."

Donna dropped her arms and stepped back. "Then, what was it?"

"As you know, we're always trying to bring business and tourists to Legacy to keep the town afloat."

Donna sighed. "Not another Gen Con. Last time, we had a dead guest."

"No. It's something you would really, really like."

Well, that was a puzzler. Somehow it involved business coming to Legacy. "It's a convention of handsome television sleuths with accents."

"Close." His eyes danced with mischief.

The man could keep this up forever. "Just tell me. I'm already upset that Alastair won the bake-off with his stupid angel food cake."

"That's it!" Mark announced with a wide grin.

"Alastair coming here with his smug little attitude. Tell me no."

The thought had her collapsing back into the wing chair while groaning. Tennyson laughed again. Another throw pillow was in reach, which she lobbed at her helper. This time she hit her target.

"I can't believe it's so hard to tell you good news. Personally, I'm surprised you don't already know. Between your mother and Janice, you know if someone has a cold before their first sneeze."

Even though it wasn't her goal to know everything that went on, she knew a fair amount, even to the point of her detective husband asking her questions about various cases when he had nada.

"Haven't talked to Mother today or Janice. She should have been at the meeting, too, but probably begged off to watch the bake-off show. "Tell me. Now. I'm not the type of person who wants to keep guessing. I don't think anyone is."

Tennyson waved as if in class. "I like to guess. I bet 'America's Next Top Model' will be filming here."

"Another close one," Mark sang out.

"No Alastair." Donna shook her finger at Mark. "No models. Remember the part about you saying I would like it."

"You will." He chuckled. "I better tell you before you're totally out of charity with me. As you know, the 'Great British Bake Off' show is very popular."

She nodded, not sure where he was going.

"Anyhow, American television producers want to have a similar show. They also want a quaint village-like town. Nora, the florist, entered our town into the running. She made some video about Legacy. Her son-in-law who works at the television station edited it for her. We watched it at the meeting, and it did look good. Anyhow, Nora got the call today. Turns out we weren't the first choice. The other city in the running was recently featured in the news for unsavory goings-on. The producer pulled the plug on that town, and we got it by default. You'll want to get busy making up signs and what all."

"When is it?"

"Next week."

"Good heavens! How do they expect us to get ready in time?"

"The other town had a six-month warning. Still, we managed Gen Con. We can do this."

The thought of a bake-off in her town had her mind racing. She tapped her temple with her index finger. "As I recall, the stinkpot of a commissioner had you busy all during Gen Con doing stupid things such as watching empty parking lots."

"True, but he's gone. I'll be able to help you more. You can call on your mother and your sister-in-law, Maria, to help. You've got Ten, too."

"That's right," Ten enthused. "What else do you need?"

"Recipes," Donna muttered, then stood and moved as if in a trance toward the kitchen. She skirted around her husband in the process.

Leaving Ten behind, Mark followed. "I don't get it. I thought you'd be excited. You'll be able to attend the actual bake-off taping."

"Of course, I will." She smiled. Her husband, despite being a very successful detective, often missed the obvious when it came to her. "I'll not only be one of the contestants, I'll also win. I might want to practice acting gracious and modest, but only after I decide on my recipes."

"I agree you're a great cook. If anyone tasted some of the tempting spreads you provide for the guests, you would be a shoo-in. I imagine this show has been in the works for a while, though, and they've already picked out the contestants carefully. There might even be some celebrity chefs in the bunch."

"There won't be." She folded her arms and hoisted an eyebrow. "Have you ever really watched the British show?"

"I've been in the same room while it was on, but there was so much chatter about ingredients or the inability to get certain ingredients that I tuned it out. Too much drama for me."

Aha! That explained all those odd answers he'd given her when the show was on. If she'd asked if a certain contestant deserved to win, he'd say she would if she made the best cake, showing he had not heard a word of her backstory.

"If…" She emphasized the word. "…you paid attention, you would know the show is about ordinary people making their best dish for the judges. Everyone has something they do very well."

"Yeah," Mark agreed. "My specialty is picking up a bucket of chicken on the way home."

The interior door swung open just in time for Tennyson to hear the remark. "Good one. My special dish is ordering pizza."

Both men laughed as if it were the funniest thing ever said. Donna didn't even chuckle.

"You two don't cook. Those who do have a trademark dish and they are asked to make it for parties and get-togethers. They've tried different variations over the years until he or she got the current version right. The dish is part of who they are. People identify them by it. It's Patty who makes the delicious potato salad, Ida who makes the icebox cake, or Norma who always brings the tired green bean casserole."

With a shrug of his thin shoulders, Tennyson said, "I wouldn't want to be associated with potato salad or green beans. Besides, the bake-offs don't give away any money. Why would you want to win anyhow?"

Instead of waiting for a reply, he ambled off leaving Donna and Mark alone in the kitchen. "If he would have stayed, I could have explained that I would have bragging rights. Being a bake-off winner would always be part of who *I* am. Maria could put it in the inn advertising. It could be on my resume, even my obituary."

"You're writing your own obituary?"

"All the smart people do. It's not smart to rely on relatives at such a time. Makes it easier on everyone. I'll pick out a photo, too."

Mark pressed a hand up against his heart. "Geesh. Do you have to talk about this?"

"No. Are you hungry?"

He chuckled. "That's right up there with asking me if I want coffee."

Donna bustled around the kitchen, filling up the coffee pot and adding decaf grounds due to the lateness of the hour. It wouldn't take her long to whip up a snack for her sweetie. Most wives might insist he fix it himself. She could, but he had suffered through the meeting for her. The least she could do was make him a snack. Besides, he never knew which items she had made for the inn and what was okay to eat. She'd learned that lesson a few months back when she told him to help himself.

"Okay. The lasagna roll-ups will be done in about ten minutes. The coffee, sooner. So, what do you know about the contestants?"

"Nothing. I assume the show brings them. Legacy's job is to keep the town commons looking green and picturesque. I wouldn't be surprised if the inn isn't booked solid. All the production crew will need somewhere to stay."

Well aware she had two couples, both celebrating anniversaries, coming in next week, she contemplated if there was a way of adjusting the dates of their visit to accommodate the production crew. Since anniversaries only happened once a year, she couldn't think of anything. What she wouldn't give to be in the bake-off.

"Mark, are you absolutely sure they have all their contestants?"

"Absolutely. What would the show be without contestants? Give it a break. You can have bragging rights in your next Christmas newsletter to all the cousins who aren't fortunate to live in Legacy."

She rested her hands behind her on the kitchen island and sighed. "I'd love to be a contestant."

Mark made his way to the coffee maker with an empty cup to await the fragrant brew. "I almost wish I hadn't told you, although Janice would have."

The cellphone chimed. Donna withdrew it from her pocket and swiped. "Hello, Janice. Mark mentioned that you might call."

"He probably thought I would call about Alastair winning. Someone must have bribed the judges. I hear the man has money."

Donna agreed while her friend tore into the latest winner. She waited to spring the news about the bake-off. Janice must not know, or she would have led with it. When a pause occurred, Donna jumped in. "Did you hear about Legacy hosting a bake-off?"

"Not that old county-fair thing. Lou Ella always wins with her brownie pecan pie. It's so sinfully good, there's never any left to display with the ribbon since the judges eat it all—every year."

"No, it's a real bake-off. A television show. They are filming it here in Legacy. I guess there will be more than one show. The crew and everything are coming here next week."

"What!" Janice shouted the word, forcing Donna to hold the phone away from her while grimacing.

"Mark heard it at the Chamber of Commerce meeting. Apparently, we were the runner up. You-know-who had a PR problem lately."

"I'm glad. Not about their PR problem, but that we snagged it. Tourism has been down with all the talk of red tide and hurricanes. I could use more people in my restaurant. I don't think people even bother to call and see if we have red tide. They assume all coastal areas are to be avoided. Not sure if the tourists are headed for the mountains or overseas."

"Hard to say. All I know is I want to be a contestant."

"Of course, you would, but I'm not sure if that's a good thing. After I got featured on the Food Channel, my business was good for a year. I mentioned the Food Channel on the menus, in the advertising, and even put up a big framed picture of me and the show's host on the wall. Didn't change any of my recipes, but I started hearing guests say they didn't think my chowder was Food Channel worthy. Before, it was delicious comfort food. I have no clue what these food snobs expect. Do you want that?"

"You know me better than that. Mark tells me all the contestants are already chosen. The only chance I have is if one of them drops *dead*."

As soon as she said the word, she knocked twice on the wooden island, causing her sweetie to give her a peculiar look in the midst of pouring his coffee. A sinking feeling came over her. The last thing Legacy needed was another inconvenient death, especially if it was murder.

Chapter Two

DONNA TEETERED ON the stepladder, clutching her end of the banner while her tall helper, Ten, didn't need any assistance to hook the banner across the front of the inn. "Almost there," she encouraged herself more than Ten as she attached her end.

It was fortunate the printing business got her banner done in time that read *Bakers, Start your Mixers*. As soon as she heard about the bake-off, she called Riley, who owned The Printing Press, and put in her order at his home number being that it was after hours. He joked that many of the meeting attendees had put their orders in at the meeting.

It irked her a little. How could she know the meeting she'd decided to skip would be the important one? As luck would have it, two of the production people would be sharing a suite and three contestants in the remaining rooms. While her culinary offerings were always delish, she would have to make them amazing. The contestants might talk them up. The production staff might photograph them and post them on social media.

Donna stepped down off the ladder and dusted her hands. "It's off to the rooms."

"Why?" Ten's brows knitted together.

She enjoyed having Ten work at the inn while he worked his way through school, but had to admit he wasn't the most inspired worker. He did what he was told—most of the time. Quite frankly, there wasn't anyone else in town who wanted free room and board and Internet, along with a minuscule salary.

If it hadn't been for Santa leaving his tricked-out truck for Ten, her helper might have moved on to a job that paid real money. It was only a matter of time until she had to hire someone else. Ten was nearing the end of his second major and would soon graduate.

"Come on." She folded up her ladder and handed it to Ten. "Put it up and I'll do an initial walk through with the gift baskets. I'll see if any of the rooms need dusting or anything else for that matter. Remember, our inn could be on television. We want The Painted Lady to put her best foot forward."

"Got it. Not sure why. One inn is as good as the next hotel," Ten grumbled as he headed off to store the ladder.

Actually, no, she wanted to say, but she didn't. It was hard to believe the boy was graduating with a double major in business and philosophy. Inns had a much harder time against hotels. While she offered a gourmet breakfast and a wine and nibbles mixer on the weekend, hotels had pools and an exercise room. They also had the sameness of every other hotel, which as hard as it was for Donna to swallow, some people liked. These were the same people who preferred the same meal in every restaurant they visited, too.

The inn had upped its game with the elevator installation. They now had a game room complete with video game systems, which was more of a nuisance than a perk. She usually had at least two pre-teen boys playing games and screaming about them in high decibels, keeping anyone else from using the room, and having the same impact on the restful atmosphere as an atom bomb. Depending on her clientele, every now and again the game system would break, or she would urge her young guests to use it in their room.

The moment she had fantasized was here. Okay, maybe she had

secretly dreamed about being a contestant. Being part of the audience in a bake-off series, not that the camera would ever pan on her, was as close as she would get to her dream. It didn't stop her from being a behind-the-scenes person. Donna entered the house and walked into the kitchen. The red flyer wagon she loaded with gift baskets sat waiting.

No hotel would have gift baskets. No, siree, Bob, only a thoughtful innkeeper would add that touch which showcased some of the industries of the town. The Wilderness Winery that squatted on the edge of town, in a moment of inspiration, had slapped on a label with a red velvet cake in the middle of the bottle, calling their table wine Bake-off Burgundy. The Chocolatier created tiny cakes in both dark chocolate and white chocolate. Franny, from Optimistic Organic Farms contributed a lavender hand cream and soap that were bound to relax the visitors. The rest of the basket was padded out with coupons and brochures from the local merchants.

In a moment of what Maria referred to as *incentive advertising*, there was a card for twenty percent off the bill for any return visits to the inn. Ideally, she would pluck the card from their fingers on the said second visit.

Noisy voices were heard on the front porch along with the sound of heavy, booted footsteps She sighed. So not ready. She glanced at a clock, which revealed it wasn't even eleven yet, so it clearly wasn't check-in time. She'd be within her rights to send whoever was here away to come back later, but that type of behavior is what a hotel would do, not a friendly local inn.

The bell rang as two jean clad men entered, toting duffels and wearing backpacks. One had a ballcap on backward while another had a scruffy beard similar to Ten's. The younger one with the cap bent slightly to put down his duffle, the word *CREW* spelled out on his t-shirt.

"Hello. Can I help you?"

The second man ran his hand through his thinning hair and smiled, causing his crow's feet to fan out attractively. "Thornton Ames. We're with 'The Majestic Bake-off.' I think we have rooms here?"

The younger guy grumbled as he tied his athletic shoe. "We didn't get in with the rest of the crew. They'll be partying every night."

Donna pretended not to hear. She reached for their key and readied her welcome speech, tweaking it the tiniest bit. "My husband, who happens to be part of Legacy's fine police department, welcomes you to The Painted Lady Inn, your peaceful haven. I was just getting ready to put your gift baskets in your room, but I can show you the room *and* leave the basket. Multi-tasking," she told them with a smile.

"Much obliged," Thornton commented with a slight drawl to his words.

"Carolinas?" Donna asked with interest. She should have guessed it with a dignified name like Thornton. She loaded one arm with gift baskets and gestured toward the stairs with her free hand. Their room was on the second floor, and they both looked capable of walking.

"No, ma'am. Georgia. Atlanta is becoming quite the production place. Cheaper than Hollywood." Thornton fell in step beside her.

"So, is 'The Majestic Bake-Off' show from Atlanta or Hollywood?" She hoped Hollywood. That would sound much more glamorous in the retelling.

The second man, who had been trailing behind them, grabbed a wine bottle from the gift basket, startling Donna. "Ah!" She recovered quickly enough not to snatch the bottle back from Mr. Grabby's hand and maintain the serene composure that a genial innkeeper would possess.

"Auggie," Thornton shot a forbidding look at his younger companion. "Have some manners."

Auggie flourished the bottle. "At least it won't be a total washout."

"Forgive my companion." Thornton confided in a lower voice. "He wasn't brought up in the South."

That was for sure. Who would name their kid Auggie? Bubba was a time-honored name among certain families, but never Auggie. Instead of commenting, she'd learned that often her thoughts were best kept to herself. She gave a sage nod as if it was understood. "What city is the company from?"

Thornton bestowed a gentle smile on her, which made his face handsome. "Chicago, ma'am."

Not what she expected, but it didn't matter if the company filmed in whatever quaint town they could find. "Oh, not what I expected. Makes me understand how you lost your drawl in the 'City of the Big Shoulders.'"

"Beg your pardon, ma'am?"

Auggie chimed up from behind. "It's from a poem by Carl Sandburg about Chicago. Don't you read?"

Auggie was right, which showed Donna you couldn't judge a book by its cover. She would have expected Thornton to know the reference. They reached the landing, and Donna walked to the room and opened it. She placed the full basket in the first room and took the pilfered basket to the smaller room. Auggie protested immediately as he followed.

"Why do I have the smaller room?"

It should be obvious to him. He was younger, so he'd naturally yield the larger room to the older adult. "Your room has a better view. You can see the beach."

"Whoa! Beach bunnies." He ran to the window and pushed the curtains aside. "Hey. A big tree blocks my view."

A slow smile brightened Donna's countenance. "I meant to say you could see the beach in late fall and winter when the trees aren't leafed out. It's a nice tree. In the mornings, a chorus of birds will gently wake you from your slumber."

The birds were not reliable for alarm clock purposes, but she couldn't resist adding that last part. Before Auggie could react, Thornton interrupted.

"We're going to have to drop our stuff and skedaddle. It's been a pleasure, ma'am. Feels like home already."

"You're most welcome, Thornton." She turned to face the younger man. "Auggie. Please feel free to call me Donna."

Auggie dropped his duffle with a solid clatter. Whatever was in there was hard and heavy. "See ya, Donna."

The young man shed his backpack on the bed and stepped around Donna without even a pardon. Thornton cleared his throat.

"He's a decent kid, talented, but he was raised up north."

She held up her hand to let him know nothing more needed to be said on the matter. Donna walked at a gentle pace as she exited the room, confident she had made an excellent first impression as a genteel proprietress.

When she hit the landing, Ten yelled up, "You got company!"

So much for their genteel image. She might as well break down and invest in the walkie-talkies Mark felt would be useful in running the inn. No way would she shout back down the stairs. Donna settled for waving madly until she got her helper's attention, then

15

descended the stairs. Both she and Maria had tried to teach Ten the check-in procedure, but he didn't want to do it. If no one else was in the hotel, he would, but that was the only time. It made her wonder what business field Ten would be best suited for, certainly not the hospitality industry.

A petite brunette and a taller man with a city haircut that screamed expensive waited at the bottom of the stairs, giving each other weighted looks. If it was one of her married couples, then the anniversary weekend was not starting out well. The woman stepped in front of Donna before her foot could reach the floor.

"I'm Emily Featherstone." The woman smoothed a hand down the skirt of her navy suit. "I believe the show booked me here?"

"Yes." Donna agreed and stepped around the woman. "I'll get your key, and Ten can show you up to your room." She put a slight emphasis on Ten's name. If he wouldn't check people in, then he'd haul them up to their rooms.

The woman moved closer and lowered her voice. "I don't want my room next to that pretender."

"Okay, but I'm not sure who you're talking about." Mentally, she sighed. While the idea of a bake-off might be fine for her, she had to accept she might be waist-high in demanding divas. That would be the price she paid. It wouldn't be the first time.

"Dalton Gallant," the woman hissed the name through gritted teeth, then shot a toxic look at the man standing a few feet away.

"How about I put you on the third floor as far away from Mr. Gallant as possible?"

"Yes." The woman pressed her hands together. "That's the first thing that has gone right for me since I was chosen as a contestant."

Personally, Donna would have considered being a contestant as one of those things that went right. The third-floor assignment used to be a punishment before the elevator. She'd give the woman the room farthest from the elevator, which might help deal with her elevated sense of worth.

She walked behind the desk, picked up a key and handed it to Ten. "Most of your information has already been filled in when the company reserved the room. You can sign the form at a later date."

"I appreciate it," the woman said and managed a superior sniff when she caught Dalton's eye.

Timing was the difference between calm and chaos. Donna waited two full breaths after the elevator doors closed on Emily and Ten before beckoning Dalton closer. With any luck, the two would avoid one another.

"Dalton Gallant," the man introduced himself. "I'm sure you guessed as much."

Not willing to confess, Donna turned the tablet they used for check-ins toward Dalton. "Put in the requested information. Do you want to use the credit card the room was reserved with?"

"Please do. I assume it was the company's card. My only expense is whatever I choose to do on the side. It's a long vacation for me on the coast, no less. The only thing that would ruin it would be the presence of my ex-wife and business partner."

"Your ex is coming here?" Donna asked, while crossing her fingers as if that would keep the woman away.

"Oh, no. She's already here. Probably in her room by now, bad-mouthing me with every step she took."

Donna's eyebrows lifted. For once she could think of no pleasant comment to employ.

"Speechless?" Dalton added. "Most people are. Our restaurant business was picked for the show about two years ago, but they couldn't get funding." He shrugged. "I thought it was all over with.

Our marriage and business were over by the time they came back. We have competing catering businesses now. Some producer or such thought it would add drama to have exes competing against each other."

Donna whistled. "It's always about ratings. Good luck to you and may the best baker win."

"That would be me." He chuckled. "I probably shouldn't say anything. I haven't met the rest of the contestants. Some of them might be outstanding. What I've seen from these shows, they have to bring in some underdogs along with a few blatantly bad cooks."

"They do that?" She had wondered how some of the people had ever made it to the finals.

He shot her a pitying smile. "Of course, they do. That's show business."

Donna turned the tablet after Dalton finished, noting his address was in Hot Springs, Arkansas. Maybe the friends she'd made on her previous honeymoon trip might know Dalton and Emily.

Right now, she knew Dalton was full of himself, and Emily was no prize. Later on, she checked in a soft-spoken older woman named Marjorie Holmes, dressed in a pastel pants suit with a floral blouse. A perfume better suited to teen-aged girls formed a cloud around the woman. Marjorie confessed her devil's food cake was sinful and got her a place on the show. Secretly, Donna knew she would root for Marjorie. The other contestants were booked elsewhere, but she assumed it was more of the same.

Drama. Drama. Drama.

Chapter Three

T HE SLAM OF the front door woke Donna. Spotting the red, glowing number 5:59 on the clock, she grumbled. "It's not even six."

Mark, her husband, who had been sleeping beside her, managed a groggy, "What?"

"Someone is banging around in the inn, and it isn't even six in the morning." The red numbers changed to 6:00. "Correction. It's now six. Who could it be?"

Mark rolled away from her, but she could still hear his mumbled answer. "Production crew."

"Why would they be up? The actual filming isn't until eleven. I inquired. Ten and I will have to whip through the rooms in a hurry if every guest has the courtesy to vacate them after breakfast. Janice promised to save me a seat in the front row. Everyone will be there."

A heavy sigh sounded, and Mark rolled back over. "Is this how it's going to be the entire six weeks of the show?"

"I imagine, if the production crew goes slamming out of here in the early hours, then yes, it is." For a smart man, her husband asked some no-brainer questions. It also could be a test.

He sighed again. "I didn't hear anyone leaving. What I heard was you announcing it wasn't six yet. It's my day off, too."

"Sorry." Even though they had been married several months, she still wasn't totally used to living with someone else. Things she was used to doing without thinking, she sometimes needed to stop and consider Mark's opinion first. For the most part, he was a very mellow individual, except when it came to the sleep he prized.

Donna sat up and slid her feet into her comfy, plaid house slippers. The best thing she could do was go prep breakfast and allow her sweetie another hour or two of sleep. She belted on her robe and made her way to the kitchen where she started with preparing coffee. Anyone who was up would want that. She was sure the production crew would love some, too. What else could they do? There weren't any all-night diners open in Legacy. There was a fast food place out by the highway where they might pick up coffee or the gas station closer to town that advertised their endless pots of brew. Donna shook her head at what horrible scenario would force her to get java at the same place she pumped gas. She couldn't think of any.

By the time she had the dining room set up, the oven turned on, and supplies lined up on the cabinet, Ten wandered in and went straight to the coffee maker.

Sighting her helper, Donna felt the need to alert him to today's tight timetable. "I'm glad you're up. We need to hustle."

Ten pointed to the coffee maker, then poured himself a cup. It was a signal not to talk to him before he had his coffee. Didn't the child understand there could only be so many coffee divas under one roof? Donna decided to switch gears.

"What's got you in a mood?"

"I'm not in a mood." He took a sip of coffee. "I'll be graduating soon, and I drove down to Charleston to interview for a job."

"I did remember." It sounded like he got rejected. Empathy wasn't her strong suit, but she did feel sorry for him. He had so much riding on that interview. "It's okay. You can stay here as long as you need to."

"Thanks. It's time for me to move on. Even you must know that." He took another sip of coffee and stared off into the distance. "By the way, I *did* get the job." He said the words very matter-of-factly.

"You did?" Donna made an attempt to swallow her surprise, but Ten's knowing expression meant he noticed.

"Didn't think I would get it?"

Donna shrugged, not knowing what to say for a change.

"Me, either." Ten chuckled.

"Why didn't you say anything?"

"They called me last night. I went by to tell Sloane, my girlfriend, first."

"I know who Sloane is."

He shook his head. "That took most of the night. First, she was excited, then she was sad. Women."

"Don't start. We've got a lot to do. As for Sloane, it will work out. You'll be little more than a few hours away."

"That's what I told her."

The back door opened and closed, accompanied by the babble of familiar voices as her mother and sister-in-law, Maria, made their way into the kitchen.

"Any unexpected help is always welcomed." Donna teased, well aware they weren't there to help since both were stylishly attired. "Your get-ups are a little fancy for work."

Her mother patted her shoulder and went to peek out the interior door. She returned disappointed. "No one is up yet. I heard you have contestants sleeping here."

"Three," Donna revealed. "Not sure how much sleeping they will do. This place is Grand Central Station."

Cecilia, her mother, poured herself some coffee and perched on an island stool. "What are they like?"

"The first two are a recently divorced couple, Emily and Dalton. Emily is a pill, demanding not to be anywhere near Dalton, while her ex acts amused by her theatrics."

Maria gave a nod and added, "He's probably used to them. What about the other person?"

"Oh, Marjorie is a sweetheart, an older lady who makes a killer Devil's food cake."

"Wonder if she's up to it?"

"Up to what?" Donna inquired. Sometimes, her family talked in phrases as opposed to full sentences assuming whoever was listening would naturally know the context.

"Oh, you know," Maria gave an airy wave of her hand. "Those tasks they're assigned. Such as making thirty-six perfect tea cakes in a very short time."

Before Donna could answer, her mother did. "Don't go thinking because she's old that she can't handle it. I imagine the woman has years of experience that enables her to compute recipes in her head and how to deal with time crunches."

A low-voiced warble and a high-pitched laughter beyond the kitchen door had Donna cutting her eyes to Ten. Familiar with the non-verbal signals, he picked up a tray of juices and water to carry to the dining room. Her mother picked up a basket of various tea bags and a plate of biscotti and followed. Time for Donna to slide the frittatas she made earlier into the oven and start the bacon.

A spate of angry words occurred on the other side of the door, then the front door slammed hard enough to rattle the bell attached to it.

Cecilia reappeared with arched eyebrows. "My goodness, you didn't lie. I'm assuming that was Emily who just slammed out of here. She popped out of the elevator about the same time a good-looking man strolled down the stairs. I told them breakfast would be ready shortly."

She placed one hand on her hip and tilted her chin up. "She said, and I quote, 'I don't have time for a sub-par breakfast.'"

"Sub-par." Donna squeaked the word.

"Wait, I'm not finished." Cecilia pointed her nose upward. "She also said, 'I have to leave early to have my hair and makeup done.'" She dropped her chin, then added, "Then the man I assumed to be her ex said she should hurry because the hair and makeup people needed all the time, they could get for her."

"The ex-husband was a good guess. Go check on him and see if he needs anything. Tell him breakfast is ten minutes away. It's actually longer, but ten minutes always sounds like an acceptable time."

TWO HOURS LATER, they were cleaning up the kitchen when Ten entered the room with a gleeful expression. "Today is going to be a wonderful day!"

Was this the same person who started out the day gloomy due to Sloane not being one hundred percent pleased with his new job? "What's made you so happy?"

He grinned. "It'll make you happy, too. I checked each floor and every room has a do not disturb sign on the door."

"Works for me." Donna untied her apron. "Give me ten minutes to get ready, and we'll head out to the show."

Maria gave her a wink. "Is it the same ten minutes we tell the guests?"

"No, it's the real ten minutes."

Donna peeked out the dining room windows as she made her way. The sun still shined, which was positive. The British show was always filming outside with plenty of greenery, and it was always sunny. She didn't know how that was possible for a country noted for its gloomy days and fog. Surely Legacy could provide plenty of liquid gold considering it was almost summer.

THE WHITE PEAKS of the event tent served as a beacon for the Legacy citizens. A temporary white picket fence surrounded the filming area. The lovely finished part faced the cameras while the crew saw the heavy sandbags resting on the supports. Janice had her purse on the seat beside her and glared at anyone who even dared to ask her if it was taken. Donna darted in front of a woman who may have decided to take matters into her hands. The result was she sat on top of Donna.

The woman popped up. "For Lands' sake! Where did you come from? I would have sworn that seat was empty."

Donna merely lifted her brows making no mention of her move worthy of any school child playing musical chairs. Before she could say anything, a young woman with a clipboard trotted by them with a finger to her lips. Not everyone had been paying attention. Several people were still talking. Finally, a man in a CREW t-shirt picked up a bullhorn and sounded the siren once to quieten down the crowd.

Once the chatter died down, the man with the bullhorn continued speaking with his voice blasting to the edges of the commons.

"You're about to witness an event in American Television. Inspired by the beloved 'Great British Bake Off' show, we decided to put our spin on it. We're calling it 'America's Best Bakers'. We were going to call it The Majestic Bake-off, but decide we wanted to emphasize the American part. It operates similar to other reality shows you may have seen with losing contestants leaving each week."

Janice leaned closer to Donna's ear and said, "I hear they actually got one of the judges from the British show."

"Really?" Donna twisted to look at her friend. "Who is it?"

Clipboard girl came around and motioned to them by putting her finger to her lips. Donna nodded she understood while Janice whispered, "Do you think that's seriously her job?"

The girl gave her a pained look and may have said something, but then there was a scream. Good heavens, what a way to start the show. Donna expected some flag waving or a beautiful child reciting a poem, not screaming. A woman attired in smock and slacks ran out of the nearby trailer. The woman babbled something to a crew member and kept pointing to the trailer.

While Donna's near vision wasn't the best, her distant vision still served. She would have sworn the woman had said the word *dead*. "Something is dead."

The woman sitting on the other side of her quipped. "It can't be the show. It hasn't even broadcasted yet." Then she guffawed as if she'd said the funniest thing ever.

No, Donna didn't think it was the show. The man with the bullhorn wandered over to where the flushed smock lady was talking with some folks in black t-shirts stamped with CREW in tall, bold letters. Some cell phones were pulled out as the now crying smock lady was led away.

Bullhorn guy was back, front and center, and said in a more somber tone. "There will be no filming today. Thank you for your interest. Come back tomorrow."

Most of the people left immediately, a few grousing on their way out about big deal movie stars and their high-handed ways. Janice stood, shouldered her purse, and glanced back at Donna, still seated. "Aren't you leaving?"

"I will, in time. Looks to me you'll have a lot of folks with time on their hands. They just might head over to your restaurant."

"Heavenly stars." She waved her hand in front of her face. "Jimmy is on host duty, and he might walk out on me if too many folks show. I gotta go."

Donna held up her hand in a distracted goodbye. She kept quiet, trying to hear what was being said across the common. It was impossible with all the noise around her. There was a good chance if something unfortunate happened, they wouldn't be shouting it through a bullhorn. A swatch of a familiar plaid showed through the open kitchen setup. Just the other day, she picked that particular jacket up from the cleaners. Mark was supposed to be off from work. Why in the world would they call him in? Unless it was an emergency or a murder. She twisted her lips as she considered that most murders would *equal* an emergency.

She got up slowly and moved toward the trailer Mark just entered. No one was watching her, which worked in her favor. The metallic clank of the gurney meant the medics were on their way. Everything would be done and gone before she made it to the trailer. She couldn't do a direct approach. Some beefy guy in a security t-shirt with his arms folded looked like he wanted to start something.

Her mama didn't raise no fools. Donna came around from behind the trailer. If nothing else, Mark would give her the details when he came home. Behind the trailer were some lawn chairs. Clipboard girl was comforting smock lady. Someone shouted for Tori and clipboard girl got up and crossed to another trailer.

An opportunity. Donna could do sympathetic when there was a

need for it. Even better, she could do Southern sympathetic, which was a whole lot sweeter and softer.

"Ah, honey." She spoke as she slid into the chair beside the woman who had managed to slow her crying to an occasional sob. Fortunately, she never left home without a clean hankie and withdrew it, handing it to the upset woman.

"Thank you."

"What's got you so upset?" Donna thought at first, she might be coming on too strong, but most women would inquire to the nature of the tears to know how to sympathize appropriately. If it were a man, the woman would be told she was much better off without that low-down polecat. If another woman had done her wrong, she'd be assured that she was a hundred times better than the Judas who stabbed her in the back. If it was job-related, Donna would mention another job was right around the corner.

The woman looked at Donna and blinked a few times. Probably searching her memory for how she knew this woman beside her. While people had no issues talking to strangers in bars, other places could be more difficult. The name Mona was embroidered in blue thread on her smock. A good chance it was her name.

"Mona, did something bad happen?"

She closed her eyes and took a deep breath. "It did. I'm the makeup artist. I do everyone's makeup before the show. I did all the contestants. I did the man last. We were joking about how difficult his ex-wife was. So, when I went to tell her she had ten minutes before the show started, I found her in her trailer, collapsed in her chair with her face smashed up against the wall."

"Oh my," Donna pressed a hand to her chest. "Was she drunk?"

Mona nodded. "I thought that at first. Here it was, early in the morning. I was upset about it, too. She messed up my makeup job, and I'd have to do it again." Mona gasped and brought the hanky up to her eyes.

"She wasn't drunk?" Donna was willing to play dumb if it got her the needed information.

"No." Mona stared straight in front of her. The only thing in view was the back of another trailer. "Before I decided to follow my dreams, I was an LPN. There was something not quite right about her neck."

"Good heavens. What was it?"

The sound of voices carried, along with the timbre of her husband's. Someone said, "Right back here. Mona was hysterical. We didn't need the public gossiping about it."

As Mark rounded the corner, she did her best to look demure.

"Donna, I should have guessed you'd beat me here."

Mona glanced between the two of them. "Do you know him?"

"May I introduce you to the finest detective in this state and possibly any other." Donna paused before she added, "My husband."

Chapter Four

MARK RAISED HIS eyebrows at the introduction. The slight twitch near his mouth meant there would be more questions later. Only an expert detective would find out what the still shaken Mona had confided to Donna. The police just didn't get it sometimes. People, especially those who had experienced something traumatic, felt much more comfortable talking to an average Jane as opposed to someone grilling them about the details.

All the stuff about where were you at 9:59? No one knows. It would be better to ask what you did after you had your first cup of coffee and go from there. Most people could describe their day, but they didn't know exactly when they did something unless they were looking at a clock at that very moment or possibly as the noon chimes of the nearby church sounded. After saying goodbye, she ambled toward the white chairs which were in a bit of disarray from the folks who had left in a hurry.

Under a sizable oak tree, her mother and Maria waited. They'd come together in Donna's car and had little choice but to wait. Her sister-in-law waved in her direction. How long had she been chatting with Mona and keeping her family waiting? It could have been five minutes or possibly ten. It was hard to say. Only a person cooking up an alibi gives exact times. A dead giveaway, Mark liked to point out, especially when the time of death was known.

When she reached the oak tree, Donna felt the need to apologize—not that she was sorry for talking to Mona. Far from it, but she did feel bad about making everyone wait. "Hey, I'm sorry about wandering off."

Her mother grinned. "Not a problem. We met one of the judges, a British gal. She might even be on that show you love."

It made her wonder who it could be. Her mother wasn't a fan, which meant she couldn't name names. A British gal could be anyone on the show who wasn't male.

"That's it? Some British female?"

Maria chuckled, sniffed a little, and a made a tiny hand wave, similar to the queen. "She was very high in the instep as if she thought a great deal of herself."

"Once again, that could be anyone. I imagine most people who have been on the show do think rather highly of themselves."

Those who didn't bake thought it was just a thing. Something they could pick up if they just followed a recipe. Not only did it take technical skill in following a recipe to a T, it also required an inherent spark, which was much harder to define.

Her mother had never been a great cook and performed very little baking. Donna had thought her sister-in-law would be somewhat better, but most of the delicious baked goodies both Maria and Daniel enjoyed came from Donna's oven. To be fair, Maria emphasized that her accounting job, along with being a mother, left little time for baking or anything more than just the most basic survival cooking. Donna also knew they brought home takeout for at least half the week, too.

Still, if someone wanted to do something, they found a way to do it. Just ask any busy female who squeezed in a yoga class or a construction foreman who was working on a deadline who still managed to squeeze in a quick game of basketball. They'd swear it was necessary for their mental health. Baking served the same purpose for her with the bonus of enriching the bed and breakfast experience.

Her mother moved closer to her and angled her head back in the direction of the trailers. "What's up with that? I knew you'd be in the thick of things."

While she wouldn't mind sharing the news, Mark wouldn't be a fan. "Police business," she confided in a low voice. "Can't say much more than that for now."

Her mother was close enough to elbow her. "Yeah, yeah, police business. You're married to a detective, and suddenly, you're a regular Columbo."

"Who?" Maria asked.

The query had Donna shaking her head in disbelief. The younger set were clueless about classic television. "He was a television detective. He was an unassuming guy that most nefarious sorts assumed wasn't too bright. It aired in the seventies, but they kept making Columbo TV specials up to 2003. I think they even had a spin-off with Mrs. Columbo."

"Oh." Maria pursed her lips. "May have heard of him. I was never a big fan of those crime television shows. Was he the one who lived in a trailer?"

"No." Cecilia and Donna answered together.

Her mother fluttered her eyelashes. "That was Rockford. Rockford Files, James Garner played him. He was my secret crush."

"Did Dad know?" Donna questioned, amused at the idea her mother had a celebrity crush.

"What part of secret don't you understand?" Cecilia teased.

"Yeah, I know. People say all the time that they have a secret crush, but everyone knows. Just like Ann-Margret was Daddy's crush."

Her mother pivoted to glare at Donna. "No wonder he wanted to watch those Elvis Presley movies. Not all of them, just the two with Ann-Margret. Called himself an Elvis fan, and I believed him." Cecilia pounded one fist into her other hand.

Before her mother could elaborate on the perfidy of her dead spouse, Maria leaned forward and tapped Donna's shoulder. "We need to move. If there isn't going to be a show, I'll need to pick up Baby Cici and finish off our taxes with my unexpected free time."

"Taxes," Donna said, but before she could point out April 15th had already passed, Maria held up her hand.

"Don't even start. I already heard enough from your brother. With his business and his somewhat lackadaisical bookkeeping records, I'm behind. However, I did file for an extension."

Cecilia headed in the direction of the parking lot and the rest of them caught up with her. After a half-dozen long strides, she asked, "Far enough away?"

"Nope." Donna glanced around expecting the town gossip to pop out from behind a tree. "In the car with the windows up."

"Ooh," her mother crooned. "It sounds juicy."

Not as juicy as she might expect. With so many pieces missing right now, the whole picture might be an entirely different story. First, she'd have to swear her family members to secrecy. It was probable the local folks hired to help set up the test kitchen would gossip. Still, she had to hold back details that would identify her as the source.

Maria would tell her husband, Daniel. Her mother would consider informing her fiancé, Simon Lightwater, not as sharing a secret, but more of explaining her day, the way information spread.

Almost to the vehicle, Donna held out her fob and clicked it to unlock the doors. The three of them climbed into the car that had managed to heat up in the short time they were gone. Before anyone could ask, Donna started the car and turned on the air conditioning. Thinking about the British show, they fussed about the heat and how bad it was for certain items such as chocolate. It made her wonder why "American Bakers" would choose a town squatting on the South Carolina border. While the coastal winds made things bearable, it didn't diminish the heat or humidity. New England would have been a better choice.

Could be the farther north you went the more expensive everything was. Those up north probably didn't have anyone like Nora campaigning for their town. It made Donna wonder what the town offered to get a show. Possibly free use of the commons, which wasn't that big of a deal. No one used it too much besides picnickers and kids tossing a Frisbee.

Donna checked the rearview mirror. She saw Heloise waving at them. "Good gravy, it's Heloise. Pretend you don't see her."

"I can't do that," her mother protested. "You know she doesn't have any real friends."

"Mother," Donna spoke, well aware of her parent's soft spot when it came to the woman. "There's a reason people avoid her. You have five minutes, no more. Remember, Maria has taxes to do. You don't want the IRS showing up on your only grandchild's doorstep."

"Absolutely not. This will only take a second. It's important to be social." The window motor hummed as the window went down on her mother's side.

The elderly gossip trotted over to the open window, exceptionally fast for someone of her years. "Cecilia Tollhouse! Exactly who I wanted to see."

"Morning, Heloise. What's on your mind?"

Donna gave the woman a curt nod, nothing more, not wanting to delay their departure. Heloise leaned into the window and swiveled her head to see who might be in the car. Satisfied, she withdrew and said, "Since it's family, I won't mince words. When are you going to marry Simon Lightwater and stop living in sin?"

Did she hear right? Donna's eyebrows shot up. "Are you living in sin?"

"Yes, she is." Heloise went on to volunteer that her mother was seen going into Simon's house at night and didn't leave until the morning.

"Good heavens, have you started spying on the residents now?" Cecilia exclaimed. "I don't have time for this. I need to go see my grandchild." The window started up, but not before Heloise got in the last word.

"You need to set a good example for your granddaughter. No one wants a hoochie mama for a grandma."

"Am I clear?" Donna asked before she reversed. As hateful as Heloise could be, she didn't want to run her down. No one would believe it was an accident. Once they got clear of the parking lot, she cut her eyes to her flustered mother. She could ask, but she wouldn't. Her mother was over seventy and could do what she wanted.

They rode in silence for a few minutes. No one even bothered to ask her about what happened on the set. Her incredible tidbit had been upstaged by her mother's love life.

Cecilia threw her hands up. "Okay, you two. I can't take you judging me anymore."

Donna could see Maria mouth 'Who me?' in the rearview mirror. She might as well second the sentiment, but her mother spoke in a flurry of words.

"It was an accident for land's sake. Does no one have anything better to do than watch me?"

"Not Heloise," Donna pointed out the obvious. "I'm sure it stings that the two of you went on a cruise together while you're the only one who came back with a beau. I'm surprised the ship crew didn't give her a thank you for leaving the party."

Her mother's lilting laugh filled the car. "So true. I just want to be clear that I am not living with Simon."

"We didn't think you were."

Maria cleared her throat. "It would be okay with me if you were. Many seniors are opting to live together to retain their late spouse's pension or full social security benefits."

"I'm familiar with that. It's not money that's stopping us from tying the knot. I guess I want something unique. I had a great life with your father, but I don't think of my relationship with Simon as the other side of the record. My goal is not to have a traditional wedding like I had before."

That made sense. Donna had used a wedding planner for her wedding who somehow thought they would want an Over the Rainbow theme. "There's plenty of wedding planners you can use."

"No, that won't do. Too much of the same." Cecilia gave her head an emphatic shake.

It's hard to know what to suggest when the person in question didn't have a clue. Maria squealed in the back seat. "I got it! You can do one of those destination weddings. Someplace exotic."

"Maybe," Cecilia replied thoughtfully, placing her index finger on her lips. She turned and stared directly at Donna.

No need to glance back. She knew what that look felt like. She'd felt it enough times in her life. Sometimes, she imagined her mother gazing at her as she was growing, fairly certain that her baby had been switched at birth. This logical, practical child could be no kin of hers. "What is it?"

"The show. You were going to give us the details."

The possibility of her mother shacking up with her fiancé had driven the thought momentarily out of mind. "Ah, that. Can't tell you too much. You know, police protocol. What I do know is one of the contestants is dead."

"Oh my!" Cecilia raised her hands to her cheeks.

"Murder?" Maria threw out the possibility. "Was it someone from the inn?"

"Don't know yet." What she *did* know was they were short a contestant. "Emily was staying at the inn. I'm just thankful she didn't eat breakfast. I don't want that to come back on me. Even better, she didn't die at the inn. Before you know it, Heloise will be calling it Hotel North Carolina, where people check in and never check out."

"Technically, she didn't check out."

"Mother, that's enough. She died. Possibly natural causes." Even though she said the words, her gut told her differently.

"Sweetie, I was teasing you." Her mother said in a consoling tone, "Besides, you have nothing to worry about. All eyes will be on the ex-husband."

Chapter Five

EVEN THOUGH IT would be a little rude, Donna needed to get rid of her mother. It was hard to snoop through the dead contestant's room with her mother going through all the reasons Heloise should be grateful *to* her instead of spying *on* her. Her sister-in-law took off immediately once they arrived back at the inn.

The only person left at the inn was Tennyson and possibly the anniversary couples. One came down for breakfast, the other didn't. Who knows where they might be now? Could be they might even want their room cleaned. First things first. She'd start a pot of coffee and send her mother on her way.

Jasper pushed up out of his kitchen bed and managed a tail wag. At least someone was happy to see her and the treats she freely gave her pet. Maybe too freely, according to the vet. How should she deal with her mother? She pondered the thought as she ground the coffee beans. After her father's death, her mother had sworn she had no interest in dating. Still attractive and outgoing, she found herself the recipient of many senior bachelors' and widowers' attention. *Vanity.* That's what she'd appeal to.

The water gurgled and chuckled as she poured it into the coffee maker. "You know, Heloise is just jealous of you. Before you met Simon, you had all the single men over sixty in the county dancing all over you."

"Some in the adjoining county, too," her mother pointed out

with a pleased look.

A tousled Tennyson ambled into the kitchen, pillow lines still pressed in his face.

Donna raised her eyebrows and asked. "Did you go back to sleep?"

"I did. Mark was here, and the kitchen was clean. No one wanted their rooms tidied." His shoulders went up in a shrug. "Why not?"

There was a half-dozen things she could say but didn't. Eventually, her helper would find out the work-a-day world didn't include as many breaks as he was used to taking. Instead, she smiled at her helper. He could do what she couldn't, motivate her mother into moving on. "We were just talking about Heloise and how she was jealous of Cecilia."

"Yeah," he agreed, wandered over to the fridge, and pulled open the doors. Donna rushed after him before he could tear into something meant for the guests. She reached around him and pulled out some pre-made pizza sticks.

"You can have these. I'll even let you heat them up yourself. You'll be on your own in a couple of months and could use the practice."

This got Cecilia's attention. "You're leaving us? Did you finally get tired of Donna's bossy ways?"

"Mom!" This wasn't working out as well as she'd hoped.

"She's not that bad once you get used to her," Ten confided. "She's all bark, no bite."

"Excuse me? I'm in the room." Donna pointed to herself, causing her mother and Ten to share knowing looks. "You know what would be great?" She slapped her hands together, forgetting her minor irritation at their teasing. Before they could ask, she'd tell them. "Mother, you could take Ten out to celebrate his new job."

She waved the wrapped pizza sticks. "Why should he make do with reheated food? Go get him something fresh."

"Sounds like a plan," her mother agreed and pulled out her phone. After scrolling through it, she announced, "I blocked off time for the show that didn't happen, I have four whole hours free. Surely we can get something tasty in that time."

"Sounds great, Cici," Ten said with a grin. His hand went up to his hair. "I should change and comb my hair at least."

"At least," Donna found herself echoing his words.

When he left, her mother reached for one of the white, stone-ware mugs she used for the inn. "Let me help you," Donna offered. She opened a cabinet and removed a to-go coffee cup. "You can take it with you."

Her mother's lips pursed into a line as she regarded her daughter. "I would almost think you were giving me the bum's rush. Still, I wouldn't mind spending time with Ten. We're only going to have him with us for such a short time. Is he going far?"

"Charleston, *South Carolina.*" She emphasized the state. There was a Charleston in North Carolina, too, and possibly a few other places.

"Oh goodie," her mother exclaimed with an impish grin. "Another reason for me to visit my favorite city and get a little shopping in."

Her mother did cut a stylish figure among the senior set. Most of it had to do with her ability to accessorize with current trends but never looking like a desperate woman trying to hang onto her youth. She eyed her mother's solid sheath set off with a floral blazer as she poured the coffee into the travel mug. Heloise probably *was* jealous.

"Here you go." She handed her mother the cup. "Does Simon know about your love of shopping?"

"Please, sweetie. There's no reason a man has to know every-thing about his beloved. Does Mark know how exceptionally tight you are with money?"

That wasn't a difficult question. They almost split up before their wedding over a financial disagreement. "He has had more than one run in with my penny-pinching ways."

The patter of large feet signaled Ten's return. "I'm ready to let my best girl take me out."

"Ooh," Cecilia cooed. "What will Sloane say?"

Ten held out his arm to her mother and said, "Let's keep it be-tween us."

She watched the two of them leave. The smooth charmer was a side of Tennyson she'd never seen. Maybe it was time for the bird to leave the nest. Donna patted her pocket to make sure she had her phone, then grabbed a cup of coffee for her journey up to the third floor. Might as well take the elevator, she never knew when the police might show up and make the room off limits. Normally, they cordoned off wherever the person died until they could determine it was natural causes.

Some deaths didn't need investigations, such as people who died in hospitals, under hospice care after a long illness, or simply expired from old age. Suspicious ones required a medical examiner. Did she even see the ME before Mark rushed her away? All she heard was the rattle of the gurney. Oh well, she'd get the information from her hubby when he returned.

The nice thing about snooping in a dead person's room was she wouldn't be expected to clean it right away. As a professional observer—what she liked to call herself as opposed to busybody or even amateur sleuth—her motto was to leave no trace behind, which meant it was time to don the gloves. Due to experience as a nurse, she'd had a chance to test some of the better brands, those similar to wearing nothing and didn't limit her dexterity. It also allowed her to use the camera on her phone, another plus.

A glance at her cat clock with the swinging tail informed her it had been almost an hour since a scream cut short the baking show. She couldn't count on things remaining quiet much longer. The contestants would be back with nothing to do and possibly the production crew members would be, too. Her cleaning caddy served as her excuse for entering Emily's room.

A Do Not Disturb sign hung on the outside of the door. Inside the room, the unmade bed, towels on the floor, and a laptop open on the bed resembled numerous guest rooms Donna had entered. There wasn't anything that stood out, but she knew one little thing could make a big difference. All she had to do was find that one little thing.

Toiletries were scattered across the bathroom vanity. The brand names Donna recognized as pricey ones. Maybe Emily came from money. One bottle was open and knocked over, oozing its over-priced contents everywhere. Her hand reached for the bottle before she forced herself to pull it back. Instead of worrying about the loss of a pricey product, she needed to focus on what it told her. Emily had plenty of money or she was expecting a big pay-off, possibly from the show.

The towels on the floor and the nightie puddled beside them indicated Emily wasn't a neat freak and that she was in a hurry. The last part Donna knew from the woman's early departure this morning.

A pair of shoes decorated the rug that led to the bedroom. Emily must have stepped out of them, confirming that tidiness was not one of her virtues. The bedside table yielded an empty soda can that had come from the floor fridge Donna kept stocked with goodies for guests. No surprise there. Beside the empty can was a prescription medicine bottle. Medicine was Donna's forte due to spending the last thirty plus years in nursing. She held up the brown prescription bottle and read the name aloud. "Paroxetine."

Odd. The medicine was often used for depression, anxiety, and sometimes to smooth out the mood swings that came with menopause. Emily was much too young for the last. If the antidepressant was supposed to make her happier, it didn't work. She checked the date on the bottle. It had only been prescribed six weeks ago. Maybe it hadn't kicked in yet. Still, Emily had to be the most aggressive depressed person she'd ever seen. Most didn't have the energy to fight with their ex.

The two of them checking in at the same place baffled her. If the Painted Lady Inn had been one of those faceless chain hotels with a couple of hundred rooms, the two would never have seen each other. She would have to make a point of asking Maria, who handled the reservations, who was paying for the room.

The open laptop beckoned. Surely, even in a hurry, the woman would have closed out of anything she had been on. She didn't expect anyone to come in so a quick peek wouldn't hurt. Donna tapped the power button with her finger, and the screen came to life displaying a document. Apparently, it'd only been in sleep mode.

The entry was headed with yesterday's date. Donna read with pleasure that Emily thought the inn was much nicer than she imagined. The words drew a picture of a much different woman.

I know I agreed to do this, but it is so hard. My job is to be a demanding diva that most people would hate on sight. My tirade about Dalton probably gave the innkeeper good reason why Dalton might divorce me. Divorcing Dalton was the biggest mistake of my life. I only wish I could have the last two years back to live over again. Things would be different. Maybe the show might draw us back together.

"You're out of time, sweetie," Donna murmured as if Emily was somewhere in the room. There was the tiniest of clicks as she aimed her camera at the laptop screen. The words were part of a digital diary. If she scrolled up, she might find out more.

The rattle of the doorknob along with cursing had Donna up off the bed in a hurry. Normally, she made it a practice of leaving the door cracked so guests would know she was cleaning. When the necessity arrived to snoop, she locked the door to prevent anyone walking in on her.

Someone wanted in. There had to be something in the room that her door rattler wanted. Something they knew Emily had or at least suspected she had. Sure, she'd like to know who felt the need to get inside Emily's room, but indecision had her frozen in place. Whoever it was would be gone by now, and it could have been a simple mistake. One of her anniversary couples could have returned to the wrong room and thought he or she had been locked out. Once the mistake was realized, the door rattler left in a hurry.

The phone was still in her hands, and she looked at the time. Mercy, it was later than she thought. She was meeting with a prospective bride in fifteen minutes who wanted to use the inn for her wedding. Donna sighed heavily. Her goal was to get people to book small weddings at the picturesque inn. Unfortunately, her prospect's appointment cut into her snoop time. There were some appetizers she needed to warm up, too, for the appointment.

Donna clicked madly at everything and anything including the open suitcase. There would be no chance to read the rest of the entries in the laptop journal. People would eventually flood the room. All of Emily's secrets would be exposed for everyone to see.

Although she initially hadn't liked the woman, Donna felt sorry for her now. Whenever someone died before living to a ripe, old age, it was easy to feel some compassion, no matter how hateful they seemed. Something was up with Emily. What Donna needed was time to read the journal, which might even give her a clue as to why someone would want to murder her.

She hovered near the laptop, not sure what to do when a marvelous idea occurred to her. Why not mail the document to herself and read it later? Her lips pursed as she pondered the possibility that it might be considered tampering with evidence.

Footsteps on the stairs catapulted her into action. She pulled up the file menu, clicked on *share*, typed in her email address, and clicked *send*. Decision made, she picked up her cleaning caddy. She took a last look at the computer and hurried back to it. A feeling told her to close the file, so she did. The police had their own hackers who would be able to paw through anything Emily typed. Would they be able to tell she sent a copy to herself? Better yet, it would look like Emily did.

Donna assured herself that Emily would have wanted it that way. If the woman died by foul means, she'd want the murderer to be found. Donna knew she was the right person to do it, along with help from her detective husband. Once she finished sending, she debated against powering the laptop down. There were probably ways to detect that. It would be more likely the battery would run out. Part of her wanted to at least close the document, but that would be interfering with the process.

She did the only thing she could do at this point. Leave. Inhaling, she mentally counted to thirty. Whoever was coming up the stairs would be gone by now. She opened the door a crack and eyeballed the area. *Nothing.* She didn't know why she was feeling so guilty. As the innkeeper, she could go into any vacant room she pleased.

Chapter Six

THE BRIDE-TO-BE SIGNED the contract with a flourish and remarked, "I know this is the right place for the wedding. It looks like it has history. If the walls could talk, I bet they'd have some stories to tell."

Donna managed a smile while inside she was rejoicing that the bride wasn't a local and hadn't heard some of the stories the inn *could* tell. This would be the showcase wedding she'd put in her brochure and on her website. They even came to an agreement that if Donna used the couple's image for advertising, the rental price would be reduced along with the couple having their pick of the photos.

The mother of the bride wanted to talk to the rest of the family about having the reception dinner at the inn after sampling the appetizers. It would be more intimate and comfortable than a public restaurant, Donna pointed out. Sometimes, she surprised herself with her marketing genius. The pleasant day invited her to walk the clients out. She stood at the edge of the parking lot and waved as the car exited.

Ten turned into the entrance a trifle faster than she liked. Her helper swung out of his truck and waved at her. "How's it going?"

"Fine, and you?"

"Much better." A genuine smile illuminated his face. "Your mother gave me some excellent advice with Sloane."

Donna hoped it wasn't the same advice *she* had received over the years. Turtlenecks are for turtles. Turning up your cuffs makes you look younger. Peach is a favorable color for natural blondes, along with rose. And her favorite: remove your makeup every night no matter what. She wasn't too sure how Sloane would receive any of those. "Oh."

"Fair is fair. I also gave her some advice on how to handle Heloise's remarks."

Normally, ten was very laid back, but he could be protective toward Cecilia, who he viewed as an honorary grandmother. "I'm sure you didn't advise her to kidnap her, drop her a couple of counties away, and see if she could find her way back?"

He gave her a strange look, then walked up to the stoop for the side door.

She'd take that as a no. It made her wonder what he *had* said. When it came to sage advice, ten was not the person she'd go to, even though he started his college career in philosophy. He used to say things like how did we know we were really here and not players in a cosmic video game. If that were the case, it must be a particularly dull game. What could he have possibly said? Better yet, would her mother actually take his advice? She waved at the dog walkers, then headed into the house.

"Ten!" she called as she entered the back hallway where Ten's tiny room, doubling as a laundry room, was located.

He stuck his head out of his room. "You rang?"

After watching the popular series with her that featured servants responding to bells mounted on the wall, he thought that a humorous quip. It probably was funny the first time, but not the numerous times afterwards. "What did you tell my mother?"

"I told her she needed to get married. Lots of people say they're going to get married. They hang out for a few years, break up, then head out in different directions. That might work for the younger set." He shook his head. "Cici isn't like that. I reminded her that she and Simon didn't have a whole lot of time left."

"You didn't." Donna covered her mouth in surprise. For once, she wasn't the one delivering home truths. No one, no matter what their age, wanted to be reminded they would not live forever. "She was okay with that?"

His brows furrowed. "I think she was. She told me I was right and wasn't certain why they were dragging their feet, although she said *she* was the one dragging."

"Hmmm," Donna tapped her cheek with her index finger. "Maybe she doesn't want to get married."

"Oh, she does." He affirmed with a nod. "She told me she wanted something different. Unique. Said at her age she should be able to do what she wanted and not be pinned in by other people's wants."

Her lips pursed as she considered if she might be part of the other people. Had she told her mother anything besides getting a wedding planner? She couldn't remember. When a wedding planner was suggested to her, she originally ignored the idea until it helped her investigate a previous wedding planner's death by murder. She exhaled audibly. "I wasn't one of those other people?"

"She didn't say," Ten answered.

Rhetorical questions were wasted on the young. "Did she say anything else?"

"Her shrimp and grits were much better than the last time she visited the restaurant."

That sounded like her mother. While she wasn't much of a cook herself, she considered herself quite the expert on restaurants and their fare. "Anything about the wedding?"

"No. She did seem happier after we talked. She even thanked me and told me I had given her a wonderful idea," Ten concluded with a slight smile. "That's all I got. If I knew you were going to give me the third degree, I would have taken notes."

He thought he was so funny. Before she could say more there was a creak of the interior kitchen door. Donna specifically didn't oil it, despite Mark's many offers to do so. Early on, she discovered that some guests treated the inn as their own home to the point of making midnight kitchen raids. It was Maria's idea to put the staff only sign on the door. It didn't help that much if they had a persistent guest. The squeak allowed her to tell if any of the guests were ignoring the staff only sign. It was an especially loud creak.

"Yoo-hoo! Innkeeper!"

Geesh, you'd think people would remember her name. She made a point of introducing herself when she met the guests. It was on the literature placed in their room *and* on the website. She held up her finger to Ten to keep that thought as she investigated what her guest could want. Sometimes, they wanted directions or recommendations.

Donna smoothed her hands over her hair before entering the kitchen only to witness a female guest peeking in her fridge. The fridge door hid the top half of her fridge invader.

"Excuse me. Can I help you?"

The woman stood and backed away from the fridge. "Yes, you can. My husband and I just woke up and would like breakfast." Possibly noticing Donna cutting her eyes to the cat clock that read eleven, the woman continued with a smile. "Your beds are so heavenly that the two of us slept in, especially after enjoying our honeymoon." She gave a little giggle that was more appropriate for a twelve-year-old than a woman who had to be in her mid-forties.

"My sweetie said he could eat a horse."

Breakfast was long past, but occasionally she made exceptions, especially for people from different time zones. "Where did y'all come from?"

"Ashville."

Not a different time zone, but truthfully, she didn't have anything else outstanding. "Any food allergies? Vegan?"

"No to the allergies. Good heavens no to being vegan. My husband is fond of saying if the Good Lord didn't want us to eat cows, he wouldn't have made them so tasty." She giggled again at her own remark.

"Alrighty, then. I'll whip something up for the two of you in fifteen minutes. Do you want coffee? Juice? Milk? Sparkling water?"

The guest appeared reflective, then announced, "They all sound good. I'll go tell my teddy bear."

Donna waited until the woman was out of the door before sighing. Giggly, older women who insisted on calling their husbands pet names like teddy bear made no sense to her. Thank goodness she was never like that with Mark. But maybe he *would* prefer her to be like that. She swallowed the repulsive idea, but maybe she *should* have a pet name for her husband like snuggle bunny or love detective. She'd try the names out when he got home.

Right now, she'd whip together an omelet, some home fries, and biscuits. If teddy bear was feeling particularly hungry, which she figured he was, a breakfast steak might not go amiss, either.

The act of cooking centered Donna. While stirring together biscuit dough, she reflected on her own life. Things were good. Running the inn had been her secret dream that kept her going whenever she had to work a double shift at the hospital. As for her husband, he was an unexpected blessing.

After Donna had passed forty, she'd given up on finding love. She had no clue that the smoky detective, who showed up to investigate the dead man in her recently purchased inn, would turn into an ex-smoker and a stellar mate. She turned the dough onto a floured board. Drop biscuits would be lighter, but people expected perfectly round biscuits.

When she started the inn, she went with what she would like to eat, but soon realized she had to give people what they wanted. Sometimes, it was bacon and home fries. Still, she rolled out the dough and cut out perfectly round biscuits. She placed them on a greased pan and contemplated her work.

"I should be in the baking show."

Jasper, who had silently watched her cook, made no reply.

It didn't matter. Sometimes, she talked to herself and definitely didn't expect an answer, especially not from her pooch.

"I don't know, Jasper, if there will be any treats for you, but I could make you a fried egg."

The puggle barked as if he understood.

Sure, it was indulgent, but Donna felt her dog could use a treat now and then. She labored on the late breakfast. Her mind turned over reasons for Emily's demise as she carefully browned the home fries. She didn't know much about the woman except she didn't like acting like a diva and was still very fond of her ex-husband, which made her question why they divorced.

The person who could answer that would be Dalton, the ex-husband. There would be no easy way to bring that up, especially now, with Emily dead. The best she could do was gauge the man's grieving. Unlike Emily, Dalton presented an easy-going façade. She had to wonder how much of it was a show.

The oven buzzer went off. Donna opened the oven, allowing the fragrant steam to escape. Golden brown and fluffy, good enough to be an advertisement for a restaurant or on a package of flour. Cooking made sense. When you followed directions, you got plump, delicious biscuits. First, she placed the heated warming stone into the basket, covered it with a linen towel, then slid the floury Southern staple in. There was a time when a woman who couldn't make a decent biscuit could never expect to marry.

Times had changed. While she *could* make an excellent biscuit, her no-nonsense attitude may have chased away suitors. Donna saw no reason to laugh at jokes that weren't funny or to pretend a man was right just to flatter his ego. Her brother called her cynical due to her fiancé deserting her at the altar when she was barely out of nursing school. Maybe that did make her less tolerant of men's shenanigans. Some men, she corrected herself. Mark was never like that.

Speaking of Mark, she hadn't heard from him. She checked her phone. Nothing. That meant he was busy. Eventually, he had to come home. Right now, she'd feed the lovebirds. Too bad she couldn't sneak into Dalton's room. Maybe he turned over his door sign to read Service Wanted. She'd check as soon as she delivered the food.

Deliver was the operative word. Ten made the mistake of showing up in the kitchen, so she sent him out with various juices, water, and a coffee thermos. No doubt the couple would want whatever possibly could be asked for. Donna assembled a tray with condiments including butter, honey, apple butter, homemade strawberry jam, salsa, hot sauce, and ketchup. Salt and pepper mills were already on the table.

Donna carried out the tray and placed it on the table where the couple were flirting with one another. "Get ready," she told the couple when they looked away from each other. "Your taste buds are going to be in heaven."

"I'm looking forward to it," the man announced. "I do appreciate your doing this for us. It's way past breakfast time. Tomorrow, we'll be on time."

"Since it's Sunday, breakfast will be served until ten," she explained with a smile.

"I appreciate the heads up." He gave her a genuine smile and gestured to his wife. "You probably think the two of us are rather silly. We were high school sweethearts but took different paths. We rediscovered each other only two years ago. Every anniversary is very special to us." He winked at her. "Try to excuse our giddiness."

Their backstory made her much more sympathetic. She tried to remember their names. "What an incredible story," she paused, hoping to pull the right names from her mental roster, "David and Kathy."

"Yes, it is," Kathy agreed and reached for her husband's hand.

The bell on the door jingled as the sound of voices filled the foyer. Most of them were masculine, but the soft modulated tones of Marjorie Holmes' voice interspersed with the males.

"I feel for you, Dalton. I heard the two of you were divorced, but you still shared a life together. When my ex-husband, Wilbur, died, I still attended his funeral. It seemed right considering we had two children together."

There went her chance to check out Dalton's room. Even more surprising was the quintessential old lady was a divorcee.

A grave voice she connected to the older crew member said, "We're at a standstill until a new contestant is found."

"That should be easy." Marjorie declared. "So many people applied to be in the contest."

"Maybe." Gravely-voice guy said. "It has to be someone who can get here by tomorrow."

If she were a cartoon character, her antennae would have just gone up. Donna strolled casually into the foyer. "Are y'all looking for a competent baker to appear on your show?"

"We are," the crew member acknowledged while Marjorie and Dalton slipped around them and moved up the stairs.

"What you need is someone who could be here in a heartbeat."

"Yup."

Donna pressed her hands together. "I bet it would be even better to have a local in the show."

"Could be." He scratched his chest. "It's not my decision. It's up to the producer. If you know someone, I could tell him."

"I know someone." Donna pointed to herself. "Too bad you missed breakfast, or you would have had a taste."

She gestured to the couple in the dining room. "How's your meal?"

"Delicious."

"Perfect."

Donna put her hands on her hips. "There you go. My recommendations."

"Give me your name and I'll give it to the producer."

Donna rushed over to the check-in table and wrote her name and number carefully on an inn brochure. Any advertisement she might get by being on the show would just be gravy. "Here you go."

Chapter Seven

DONNA COULDN'T BELIEVE she was going to be on television. Nothing could ruin her good mood. It wasn't a done deal, but almost. Once Thornton gave her name to the producer, it should be a done deal. After all, where else would they find a ready-made contestant?

She practically floated to the table where her happy couple sat. "Anything I can get you two? If you're still hungry, I'll be happy to make you another tasty treat."

Kathy smiled. David patted his stomach. "It's a tempting offer, but every yummy morsel goes right to my spare tire."

"Oh, sweetums, that is so untrue. You're in great shape. Almost the same as when you were in the Green Berets."

The wife cooed the words. Okay, maybe listening to the lovey-dovey couple overly long might ruin her mood. "Well, if you don't need anything, I'll be in the kitchen." *Throwing up*, she mentally added.

Doing breakfast dishes for the second time today wouldn't bother her. She'd get the pots and pans done first. Surely, by then, Kathy and David would be done, and she could get their dishes.

Tennyson drifted into the room while she was scrubbing the skillet, a good deal more somber than he was earlier. He plopped down on one of the island stools and sighed heavily.

Lord, have mercy. She knew what that sound meant. Where was

Mark when she needed him? Ten would sigh several times until she asked him what was wrong. She'd ask. He'd tell her and ask for advice. After being asked, she'd give him practical advice, which he would ignore and go ask someone one else. Why did she bother?

Instead, she put some extra effort into scrubbing the skillet. Potatoes tasted best when cooked in cast iron. After rinsing it, she heaved the skillet back onto the stove and turned on the burner just enough to dry it. Before she could get around to seasoning it, Ten sighed again, even louder. She wouldn't be surprised if Kathy and David stopped making cow eyes at each other to wonder if the inn might be haunted.

"What is it?"

Ten shot her a world-weary look and leaned against the island. "Sloane thinks if I really loved her, I wouldn't take the job in Charleston. Instead, I'd stay here and go to graduate school to be with her."

"Does she now?" Donna wiped her hands on a dish towel, then crossed her arms. "Did she explain how you would afford graduate school?"

Tennyson melted a little more on his stool. "She thought I could get a scholarship."

A derisive snort escaped Donna. "That would be nice. I imagine lots of graduate students would be all over that. The truth is most folks that go to graduate school are doing it at night and working a regular job in the day time. A few might even get help from their employer, but still work all day, and go to school at night. There are a few who have indulgent parents who pay their way through graduate school. You think your parents would do that, considering how long it has taken you to get your bachelor's?"

"No. As for how long it took me, keep in mind most kids take five years to graduate. I just took a bit longer. I didn't flunk any classes, which is a plus."

She didn't want to pile on too much when he was already down. She strolled over and gave him a half hug, then dropped her arms as she spoke. "Don't worry too much. Sloane is being emotional. She's afraid she'll be left behind, and your head might be turned by all those Southern Belles."

He forced a laugh. "That won't happen. It hasn't happened here."

"I know," Donna agreed, and Ten shot her an irritated glance. Speaking the truth tended to be her specialty, but she had to learn not to give it to people all at once. "What I meant was *you wouldn't* be interested in those Charleston flirts."

"Okay." He narrowed his eyes just enough to express doubt. "Go on. How is anything you said so far helpful?"

"It's the truth. No one is standing on the corner giving out scholarships for graduate level work. If there were, more people would have stayed for their graduate degree than going to work. It's common sense for you to take the job you were offered. Most kids don't even get a decent job, especially if they have a liberal arts degree. They count themselves lucky to manage a fast food restaurant. Surely Sloane has common sense and can't argue with the truth."

"I don't know." He shook his head. "When you say it, it sounds good. Believable."

"It's the truth." Still, the truth usually never won any popularity awards. "Here's a non-practical suggestion. Find a way to show her how much you care." A thought inserted itself. "Unless you don't. Maybe moving to Charleston is a way to get out of an unsatisfactory relationship."

Ten pushed off from the island. "Not you, too. I have to get to class to present my final project."

"Good luck. You'll be great." She honestly hoped he would but doubted it. If he could compartmentalize his heartache, he'd be golden. It hadn't been her intention to add to his distress. The possibility of Ten wanting to leave popped into her head. He could want to go someplace where no one knew him. Instead of being the failed philosophy major, he would be the up and coming business-man. Besides, could a person truly fail philosophy? It was only one person's opinion. Should it matter if a person didn't truly exist but only thought he existed? Good heavens. Here she was quoting the nonsense Ten used to spout that had her shutting herself into closets to keep from laughing in his face.

There was not much more she could do. Sloane would probably appreciate things spelled out for her. Maybe even schedule times when they could get together. She'd mention it to Ten when he got back. The clean-up took another thirty minutes or so before her kitchen gleamed the way she liked it. As she passed the kitchen window that looked out on the front, she witnessed Maria's car turning into the driveway. That was odd. Her sister-in-law men-tioned spending the day catching up on taxes. Oh well, she'd find out soon the reason for the unexpected visit.

The back door slammed, and she heard the infectious cooing of her niece. Donna hurried down the hallway to greet her niece and sister-in-law. "Oh, you brought me my favorite niece."

"She's your only one." Maria reminded her and allowed Donna to take Baby Cici.

"True, but even if I had more, she'd still be my favorite." Donna turned her attention to her niece, who was decked out in a frilly yellow dress and white socks with ruffles. "Don't you look special?

What's the occasion?"

"Pictures. She's ten months. We try to capture every month with a photograph. Babies grow so quickly. Before you know it, she'll be walking."

As the only grandchild and niece in the Tollhouse family, Donna doubted if Baby Cici's feet had ever touched the floor. "She has to get some crawling in and pulling herself up before moving on to walking."

Maria crinkled her nose. "Look at you. A regular child expert. When she's at home, she has plenty of time to practice while I'm doing taxes. As for pulling up, she's pulled several things *down*. Anyway, I didn't come to talk about her walking progress."

Donna made faces at the baby, causing her to chuckle. "Of course, she didn't. Your mama wanted to show off how precious you are. You are so very special."

"Yes, she is." Maria smiled. "That's not the reason I came over. Turns out I couldn't do the taxes today." She wrinkled her nose. "Vital receipts are missing. Daniel is in search of them. I figured I had the day free, so I'd take the baby to Lloyd's Photo Carousel. My plan was to stop by Cecilia's to show her how cute Cici looked in the dress she bought. Only problem was, she wasn't there, but her car was.

AARP should use her mother on the local edition of the magazine. She was the most active senior anyone knew. She also was the most stylish. "You know how she is. One of her friends or Simon could have picked her up."

"Normally, I'd agree. Dorcas, who lives to the right of Cecilia, asked me where my mother-in-law took off to. Said she saw her get into a car and a strange man put a suitcase in the trunk."

"That's peculiar. Mother never mentioned a trip. The neighbor must be confused. Occasionally, she calls an Uber when she's unsure of a location. That's all it is."

"I hope so. I called her twice and no answer."

Donna shrugged. Her mother not answering the phone wasn't too unusual. Sometimes, she didn't know where her phone was, or it was off, and occasionally, the battery was dead. "It doesn't help that she has a brand-new phone. Maybe the sound is off."

"You're right. I'm afraid I overreacted. Thank goodness I stopped here before heading home and worrying Daniel. To think I was upset due to the blinds being closed."

"The blinds were closed?" Her mother was a big proponent of sunlight. She used to wake Donna in the morning by flinging her curtains wide to flood the room with sunlight. At least the daylight savings time switch allowed her to stumble out of bed without the bright sunlight a few months out of the year.

"Yes," Maria answered, her brow furrowed. "I thought it peculiar, but maybe she was trying to prevent sun damage to her furnishings."

"Some might," Donna agreed. "The front room is her white room, the one with the white furniture and the pale beige carpet with tiny pink rosebuds on it. There isn't much to fade in that room. Besides, Mother is a big believer in the power of sunlight as a mood elevator. She only shuts the blinds when she goes to bed. Part of it is to shut out ambient light. The other reason is to let people know she's retired for the night. We had a rule that none of her friends had better come knocking after the blinds were closed, but there *was* another reason she'd close the blinds."

Baby Cici reached in her mother's direction, who took her and walked over to the island to sit down on a stool. She sat with a sigh. "I'm ready for this chunk to start walking. I bet I know the other reason. Your mom is closing the blinds to keep Heloise from spying on her."

"Ha!" Donna waggled her eyebrows, causing Baby Cici to coo. "That's a good one. My mother wasn't meeting men in the front room while I was growing up. She had no reason, then, to shut the blinds. I remember on the few family vacations we went on that Mother went around locking the windows and closing the blinds. She was afraid burglars might do some window shopping. In retrospect, we really didn't have much that was worth stealing. My father always humored her about her security check."

"Did she say anything about leaving?" Maria had one arm firmly wrapped around her child and rested the other on the island top. "I mean, it's not like she couldn't jaunt off somewhere. I'm just surprised she didn't tell us. Not a hint."

Donna held out her hands. "I got nothing. It's not like Mother to be so secretive. Usually, she'd give us details about the trip: where she was going, who she'd meet, the address and phone number where she was staying, in case something happened to one of us. Not like her at all. It's more like the behavior of a youngster who'd take off on a whim and forget to mention it to his parents." The mention of youngster caused the proverbial lightbulb to shine. "Ten."

"What does Ten have to do with this?" Maria shook her head. "Are you sure you're not just grasping at straws now?"

A senior taking advice from someone who hadn't even experienced the full roller coaster of hills and valleys that life had to offer did seem strange. "I don't know. Ten came home all happy after he and Cecilia exchanged advice. I have no clue what Ten could have told her."

"Is he here? We could ask him."

"He had a class. I wouldn't worry overly much. He's not exactly a wild card. Any other guy would have moved out of here long ago. Personally, I think staying at the inn was a safe place for him."

"Of course, it was. It was his home away from home. He had food, a room, cable, and people who are willing to pay attention to him. Most kids would like that even if they wouldn't admit it. By working at the inn, he scored a free truck from Santa, too."

"True."

Maria pushed up from her position to change supporting arms around the baby. "And, he has some great stories to tell."

"My bottom line would be much better off without his storytelling. He's not a wild child. He's unlikely to suggest sky diving or joining the circus."

"You're right. Besides, most circuses have folded up their tents. Still, sometimes Cecilia hears what she wants and interprets things the way she wants them to be."

Donna took years to figure that out, while her sister-in-law surmised it in only a couple. "You're right. The possibility of what mother might do makes me nervous. The best thing for anxiety is…" She left the sentence hanging to see what Maria might say.

"Chocolate."

Donna sucked her cheeks in. Cooking would have been her answer, but chocolate worked, too. It also didn't mess up her clean kitchen. "You're in luck. I happen to have some emergency chocolate."

Maria wrinkled her nose. "I know."

Chapter Eight

DONNA CARRIED A tray of canapes to the dining room where the two married couples and show crew members were enjoying free drinks and eats. The conversation and laughter grew louder as she entered the room and not just because she was closer, although that did have some influence.

Tonight was the time for her scheduled mixer. It was part of the weekend package. For a moment or two, she thought about not having it due to the death of a guest. No one knew Emily with the exception of her ex-husband, who wasn't engaging in the frivolity. It made her wonder if he was attached to his ex-wife as much as Emily was to him.

"Fresh from the oven. Hot cheese and onion tartlets, brie and cranberry tarts, mini-macs, plus holiday bacon appetizers." The last was merely a strip of bacon wrapped around a chunk of parmesan sitting on a club cracker. It was always a crowd pleaser, except with the vegetarians. Since one incident, food preferences and allergies were part of every reservation form.

A few cheered, but they all crowded around as soon as she set the tray down. The normal process was to have little nameplates identifying each item, but with the way things were going, it fell by the wayside. She could have made them instead of texting her husband endlessly. Mostly, she got nothing for her efforts, which did aggravate her at the beginning of their courtship. Mark explained that he could be grilling a suspect and couldn't stop to reply to a text. Finally, around six, she got a text. *Be home late. Love you.*

Personally, the mixer was as much for her as it was for the guests. One of the things she learned early on in the hospitality industry was the power of reviews—even bogus ones. One guest had ranted about a room being too pink. The last thing she needed was someone to complain about having no mixer when it was clearly mentioned in the brochure and on the website. It was one of the things that set her apart from the faceless chain hotels.

Tennyson handled the beverages. He had donned a button-down shirt and dress pants. Even his hipster beard was trimmed, making him look more professional. To think, when she first hired him, he wasn't even twenty-one. Now he stood by the mobile bar, which was a rolling cart that had a wine glass rack. It didn't need to be very big. All the inn served was sodas, wine, and a local hard cider. She did have a permanent sign that reminded everyone the drink limit was two when it came to liquor.

The sign worked better than trying to remind Tennyson when dealing with the guests. Mark had better luck. He usually managed to work in the fact he was a local law enforcement officer when someone insisted on a third drink. Sometimes, he suggested a restaurant and bar that was within walking distance. Some people assumed that meant a block away, but it was really a half mile, a nice walk on a pleasant evening.

Donna scanned the room before going back to get the rest of the eats. Marjorie was missing. She had returned with everyone else, but she could have had other plans or just didn't feel the need to socialize. Not everyone does.

They had started the night with some classic appetizers, includ-ing chicken wings, crudités with dip, and a deviled egg spread, which was deviled egg spread on toasted crostini. Maybe she went a little overboard, but that's what happened when she had too much to consider.

For dessert, she made another all-time favorite, brownies. Also, on the menu were key lime tartlets and fresh fruit salad. If anyone was watching their weight, they would have to settle for nibbling on the raw vegetables and a chicken wing or two. The way she saw it, none of the portions were that big. She wouldn't be surprised if a few people actually went out to dinner afterward.

So far, she hadn't heard much information about Emily's demise, although she tried to plant herself in various listening areas with a feather duster in hand. The crewmen took advantage of the entertainment lounge to play some video games. Instead of talking about work, they trash talked one another about who might win. What a waste of fake dusting.

Instead of dropping the desserts and high-tailing it out of the dining room, she decided to pass them out herself. It would give her time to interact with the guests and make sure no one took more than two, depriving another guest of the tasty treat. She had made enough for Dalton and Marjorie. One or both might still drift down in search of food. Knowing people, the way she did, she made them plates and left them in the kitchen.

She slipped into the kitchen and hoisted up the heavy silver tray she'd already decorated with individual plates loaded with the three desserts. Her intention was to give each person a plate, then she'd go back for the second plates. This time, she'd be more welcome and might engage in chit chat or hear something pertinent. Her plan worked. When she strolled over with the second helpings of the desserts, her crew guys were talking about the show.

"Yeah, he wants us there at seven. The show *is* going on, which makes me happy. I'm a fan of eating on a daily basis."

The older crew guy, Thornton, said, "Me, too."

"I guess you need the job more than me, since you have all those ex-wives."

Auggie chuckled, but the other crew member didn't appear amused.

"I only have two ex-wives and two children. It's not all that many, but it does get expensive, especially on my salary."

This conversation wasn't benefitting her. "Dessert?" she inquired and displayed the tray. They both helped themselves to a plate, while the younger guy grabbed a second. That meant for her to be able to make another sweep, someone would have to give up a dessert plate she had waiting in the kitchen. Hopefully, it would be Dalton or Marjorie and not Tennyson or Mark, whom she had also made plates for. Obviously, the men weren't going to talk while she was there, which meant she had to wade in.

"I couldn't help but hear the show is up and going again. I know the city of Legacy will be glad to hear that."

"Yep," Young and Hungry answered with his cheeks packed with brownies.

She didn't see the brownie go in, so she couldn't analyze if he could swallow it whole like a snake could an egg. All she knew was a full-sized brownie vanished from the dessert plate. Those two wouldn't win any conversational awards. The ball was back in her court. "Did you get a chance to give them my name as a contestant?"

"Sorry." The older man shot her an apologetic look. "I was told they already had a contestant—someone who was well known in the town for being opinionated and colorful. It makes the producer happy. He's sure it will cause drama. That's what keeps the viewers watching."

"Yes," she found herself agreeing. If she left the conversation now, it would look like she was in a snit. She was. How did Heloise get into the show? She couldn't even cook. "Do they ever bring in folks who can't cook, for comic relief or such?"

The younger one gobbled his desserts with glee, even to the point of trying to steal his associate's brownie and got his hand slapped for the effort.

The older man rubbed the back of his neck as he gave the matter some thought. "It's the first show, so it's hard to say how good of a cook each contestant is. A few may have lied about their skills. It would make better television to have them evenly matched, but I imagine a few will choke due to being watched."

Tennyson gestured in Donna's direction. Thank goodness for that. It would serve as her exit. "Been nice talking to you. Good luck with the show."

Cookie monster laughed, spewing crumbs. "As long as everyone stays alive, we're good."

Not knowing how to respond, she smiled, then strolled over to Ten. "What can I do for you?"

"I need a restroom break. Can you stand guard on the bar? Everyone has had their two drinks." He dashed off before she even agreed.

The easiest way to handle the issue was to push the cart back into the kitchen. No one would be expecting any more free beverages with the cart gone. Sweet tea and iced water sat on the server along with glasses. She placed the extra desserts on the cart and pushed it into the kitchen. There was some grumbling. It was to be expected. Her profit margin was slim as it was. All she needed was for someone to trash the sheets or room, and she would be in the red.

Maria, always good with passive handling of destructive guests, posted online, in the brochure, and on the tastefully framed placard in each room that guests were financially responsible for the destruction or disappearance of items in a room. She added on that guests should keep their rooms locked just in case they thought they could peddle some story about a homeless man wandering into the room and spilling red wine on the white down comforter.

At least she didn't include an inflated price list of how much everything cost just in case a person felt the need to take a comforter, pillow, or minifridge with them. It might be smart legally, but Donna just thought it was tacky. A shame that she had to give the notice with every reservation, but after replacing two sets of five hundred count sheets, she had no option.

Inside the kitchen, she took a deep breath and closed her eyes briefly. Her back hurt and her shoes were too tight. When she opened her eyes, the extra laden dessert plates sat on the island, reminding her of her plan. Yeah, she should go see what she could find out. Instead, she pulled out a stool, sat, picked up a brownie from a plate, and bit into it.

Ten wandered in and eyed the cart. "I should have thought of that. Are we done for the night?"

"I am. I saved back food for you and Mark."

He grinned. "Sweet. I'll miss the food when I go."

She arched her eyebrows at his comment.

"I'll miss you, Mark, and Jasper," he added.

Donna noted the food got first billing while she and Mark were grouped with the dog. As if on cue, Jasper stepped out of his basket and stretched. Ten wasn't the only one who expected treats after a mixer. "No worries, fellow. I saved you some bacon."

"Um," Ten cleared his throat. "The bacon on the paper towel

was for Jasper?"

Sometimes, she thought Ten was an adult male ready to strike out in the world and others that he somehow missed out on the obvious. More likely, he pretended not to know. Jasper would never go without. His rounded tummy attested to that.

"Yes, it was. Did you think I laid it aside for anyone who might be passing through the kitchen?"

He shrugged, then grimaced. "It sounds stupid when you say it that way. I wasn't thinking." Ten turned to the puggle, "Sorry, Jasper. You can have my bacon appetizers."

Donna picked up two appetizers from the plate she made for Tennyson and gave one to Jasper, who wolfed it down. He wagged his tail and looked up at her hopefully until she delivered the second treat.

"I can't believe you did that. You gave my food to the dog."

"You ate his. Fair is fair. Welcome to the real world."

He blew out a breath. "You're right. I should have asked.

The fact he looked so woebegone and he'd be gone soon made Donna extract a bacon appetizer from both Dalton and Marjorie's plates and add it to Ten's. Besides, they'd never know. By this time, she imagined they weren't showing.

Ten took his plate. "I appreciate it. I know I don't deserve it but I appreciate it just the same."

His comment made her chuckle. "Sometimes you get what you deserve. Other times, you don't."

Ten opened the microwave and stuck his food in it.

Before he could hit the power button, Donna scurried over to the microwave and grabbed the door. "Good heavens. Didn't I teach you better? That will make the puff pastry a soggy, inedible mess. Use the toaster oven."

"It takes so long." There was the tiniest whine in his voice. "I need to talk to Sloane."

In Donna's observations, the younger set could do almost anything with a phone in their hands and often did. "Take the plate to your room and call her."

"I need to talk to her in person. It's hard to make a grand gesture over the phone."

"Grand gesture?" She had heard *that* phrase before.

"Cici suggested it."

That explained it. "Come to think of it, what did you tell my mother anyhow? We haven't found hide nor hair of her."

"Oh, that." Ten put his plate in the toaster oven and turned it on. "I told Cici if Heloise was making noise about her not getting married, then she should prove her wrong."

Donna pondered the advice. "Basically, you told my mother to elope?"

"Yeah, I guess so." Ten leaned back against the counter. "I'm not sure what the big deal is. She and Simon were planning to get married, and they're not getting any younger."

"True on both accounts." She held a hand over her heart. "I think my mother has eloped. Two senior citizens headed to who-knows-where to get married."

"On the upside, they're not underage."

She poked him. "Who knew you were a comedian?"

The side door slammed, causing them both to look up. Mark came in through the back hallway. "What a day and it was my off day, too." He sighed heavily and pulled out a stool. "Please tell me you have coffee and food."

"Always." Donna scooted over to the coffee maker to make a pot of decaf. She smiled in Ten's direction. "I can bring that to you when it's done."

"Got it. Code for you want to be alone."

"Something like that. I appreciate your understanding." She gave a finger wave, sending Ten on his way. She counted to ten after Ten left before turning to her husband. "What's up with Emily? Did she die from sheer happiness due to being a contestant?"

Mark shook his head and somehow managed to appear more careworn than when he entered the kitchen. "Not unless happiness can snap your neck like a wishbone."

She was right! It *was* foul play, but suddenly Donna didn't feel the least bit triumphant about the fact.

Chapter Nine

EVEN THOUGH SHE was dead tired, sleep wasn't going to come easy. Mark helped her pick up the dining room, then headed to bed. Donna set the tables for the morning, not sure who would show for the meal. By the time she entered the bedroom, Mark's snores were going full steam. *Drats.* She'd hoped to pump him for more information other than the medical examiner arrived and pronounced Emily's death from asphyxiation, which made sense since she couldn't breathe. More than one car wreck victim arrived in the hospital with a broken neck. The difference was they were more likely thrown clear of the car and were in a prone position that allowed them to breathe—not so with Emily.

Apparently, the show was still going on, despite a suspicious death. She stared at her husband's sleeping form and debated if she should wake him. He wasn't at his best when she woke him, and he might mutter that he couldn't tell her anyhow. Mark could be in his everyone-is-a-suspect mode. The most innocuous-seeming people were always the killer in all the crime dramas.

Instead, she lay on top of the covers still attired in her clothes thinking about Emily moments before her neck was broken. She's already had her makeup and hair done and was waiting for the signal to be introduced to the viewers. From the short time she'd been surrounded by trailers, she noticed they all seemed to have only one door. Wasn't that true of all trailers? It wasn't like she was an expert on them.

The numbers on the clock radio glowed red, reminding her it was almost midnight, which would explain her exhaustion.

Still, she could use her phone to look up trailers. Donna kicked her shoes off with a sigh and perched on the side of the bed. *Trailers,* she typed into the search bar. What she got was trailers to haul dirt bikes, snowmobiles, and cars. There were a few with open metal work that were better suited for lawnmowers. Not what she wanted. People referred to them as trailers on the lot. Maybe she should try *camper.*

Travel trailer was most similar to what was on the lot. It was a vehicle that was hauled there, put into place, the hitch was unlocked, and it was stabilized. According to the trailer website, a person needed tire chocks, blocks on stands for the tongue, leveling wedges, and there was a metal contraption you could buy called the *stabilizer*. She wasn't sure if these trailers had all that though. A field trip would be required. She never ascertained from looking at the few trailers she saw if they had one or two doors.

A message showed up at the bottom of the website. It read, *what type of trailer are you looking for.*

The clock now read five past midnight, so she was pretty sure no one was up manning the local trailer website. Ten mentioned most of those popups that showed up whenever you stayed on a merchandise website too long were just automated and not real people. Robots or maybe a computer that answered your question could provide real information without the heavy sales pitch. Donna slowly typed in *need small trailer for movie set.*

The answer came back fast. *We don't have those.*

Who knew this was a specialty item? Donna knew it was a long shot but decided to type in another question. *Who does?*

Celebrity Trailers in Atlanta, Georgia.

Odd. She hadn't expected an answer. Most companies aren't quick to send you to another company, but this was a machine, not a person. It wasn't working for a commission. A few clicks later and she was onto Celebrity Trailers. Mark murmured something about the light. She clicked it off and stretched out on the bed. Her intentions were to look at the site, then get up and get ready for bed.

The site featured shiny trailers specifically for movies. Some were for wardrobe. Others were for hair and makeup only and featured big lighted mirrors. The one labeled Single Star not only had a kitchen, a bathroom, and a plush living room, but it also had a huge widescreen television and a fireplace, which she assumed was propane. A person could live in there. None of them at the commons were that fancy. It also brought up the idea that trailers were normally shared. Emily didn't merit a trailer on her own. Who could have been her roommate?

She scrolled past one entitled Honey Wagon, which was a mobile restroom. Finally, she found a clear photo of the front of the trailers. Some had one door when it was the matter of a star waiting inside. Those who shared a trailer had walls separating the suites. The ones that expected many people passing through, such as wardrobe, had two doors on the same side of the trailer, but at different ends.

What had the trailers looked like on the set? None of them were this fancy. She clicked on *reserve* but saw no prices. Her eyes flickered closed as she considered the fact no prices were listed. The next thing she heard was a phone ringing.

Her eyes opened slowly to stare at the clock radio. It was only six-thirty. Who could be calling at this time? Donna glanced down at her phone. It wasn't ringing.

Mark rolled over and grabbed his phone that he had left on the bedside table. "Taber here."

Good heavens, she hoped it wasn't another murder. Her husband scooted up into a sitting position, suddenly alert, and cut his eyes in her direction. "Got it. No problem. She'll be there immediately."

The fact he looked at her and said *she* made her more than a little curious. Mark hung up the phone and smiled at her.

"Guess what?"

Did anything good ever start with *guess what*? "I'm afraid to guess. Just tell me."

His eyes surveyed her outfit but made no mention that she still was attired in yesterday's clothes. "The show needed a new contestant fast. I told the producer you would be willing, and you're a good cook. You were supposed to be there ten minutes ago."

She leaped out of bed and thrust her hands through her hair. "Look at me. I'm a mess."

"That's what hair and makeup are for. You know the general location?"

"I do." Part of her danced and shimmied with excitement. She, Donna Tollhouse, would be a contestant on a bake-off. It would be free publicity for the inn. Yippee! Another part of her was irritated that she didn't get a chance to plan ahead. "Mark, couldn't you have told me this earlier?"

Not waiting for an answer, she opened the closet door to find something that would strike the right balance between upscale and folksy. They probably wouldn't provide a wardrobe so she would have to make do with what she had. If she had known, Donna could have hit the mall.

"Meant to," Mark offered and shrugged. "Murder has a way of

overshadowing everything.

"Why are they still having a show? I would have thought you would have shut it down." Donna picked out a green pants suit Maria had once told her was slimming. If the camera added another ten pounds, she'd need the slimming effect.

"That was my first choice. The city council must have been whispering into the commissioner's ear. He decided only Emily's trailer is a crime scene. The show must go on, and the town needs its shot of fame. I could have told you something like this would happen when we let in movie people."

His rant was muffled as Donna pulled off her shirt to don another. Oops, she forgot her deodorant. It would be a definite need, today of all days. As much as she loved her husband, he could be a bit paranoid about anyone who wasn't a local. The tourists the town subsisted on brought their big city ways with them and possible crime. After no less than seven murders in Legacy since she met Mark, he might have a point.

"I need you to start breakfast," she informed Mark as she dashed past the bed.

"Can't I call your mother? She loves to do that stuff."

He was right about that. Sometimes, Donna worried if she gave her mother a little responsibility, then she'd take over the inn and run it the way she thought it should be. "Can't. My mother has taken off for parts unknown."

The revelation caused Mark to struggle into a sitting position. "What?"

She didn't have time for this. "She was last seen putting a suitcase in the trunk of an Uber car. Furthermore, she's not responding to messages or calls. Maria and I assume she's with Simon."

"Doggone it, woman, you're not even worried!"

Oh no, he didn't. Donna shot him a look that should have incinerated her husband on the spot.

"Oops. Sorry about saying *woman*." His flushed cheeks testified to his embarrassment. "I'm just worried about Cecilia."

Her reply was a grunt. As apologies went, it didn't wipe out the fact he grouped her with every other female on the planet. She had a name, and he knew it. "I'm worried, too. She's an adult and not senile. No reason for us to be in her business, but if you had time to dig around, I'd appreciate it. I'd check airports, first. Mother kept saying she wanted something original for her wedding. For all I know, they're going to climb a mountain peak to say their I Do's."

Donna didn't wait for a response. She didn't have time.

EVEN THOUGH THE sun was barely up, there was a bustle at the commons. Cars crowded the street as Donna searched for a parking space. She sucked in her lips as she made a slow survey of any possible spaces. A honk behind her had her gritting her teeth.

"Keep your pants on," she grumbled, then turned into a gloriously empty space. "Take that, honker!"

Normally, she didn't experience much road rage, but today didn't classify as even close to normal. She was having the opportunity to live out a dream rated high on her bucket list. She inhaled heavily. It would have helped if her husband gave her the opportunity to prepare for it. One thing she wouldn't have done was stay up most of the night searching for movie trailers. With any luck, the makeup people could erase signs of the sleeplessness.

After parking the car, Donna shouldered her purse, then paused before closing the door. Would it be better to leave it in the car? Would she even need her purse? Obviously, everyone and their cousin would want to be on the show. There might even be an entire line of Donna Tollhouse pretenders lined up to get their chance at baking fame.

Driver's license was a must along with her breath mints. The purse would have to go. No bakers showed up with a purse. It made them look as if they were either ready to leave or just wandering in off the streets. Car keys would be an issue. With her big wad of keys, it would create a popcorn ball size bump in her already frumpy garb. Surely her purse would be safe in the trailer. The thought was replaced by one that featured a dead Emily. *She* wasn't safe in her trailer. Donna didn't have a chance to ask if anyone heard signs of a struggle. The only scream the audience heard was from the makeup artist.

She pushed the key fob and locked the car. Being on the show would be wonderful in so many ways. It would allow her close contact with the crew, not something she'd necessarily have on an ordinary basis. Since she was on the show, her questions might not sound too nosy. Her lips twisted as she speed-walked through small clusters of folks drinking coffee and talking. Most wore black shirts emblazoned with the word CREW in big white letters.

Donna stopped when she realized she had no clue where to go. In her rush to get here, she forgot to ask Mark. The skinny clipboard-wielding girl from the day before glanced down at her list and asked, "Are you Donna Tollhouse?"

"I am." What could this young person want?

"You're late!" The woman glanced down at her board. "You needed to be in makeup thirty minutes ago." She gave Donna another look. "Yes, you would have benefited from the extra time."

Mercy. Were they teaching young folks that they thought they could get away with being so rude to their elders? The girl could do with some instruction, but she needed to be in makeup. "Point me to the makeup trailer."

The girl gestured to the group of trailers squeezed into the edge of the commons. Well, that was no help. Makeup could be any trailer except the one wrapped in yellow police tape. By the time Donna turned back around, clipboard girl had moved on to insult someone else. As an intelligent female and stellar sleuth, she could figure it out on her own.

As she got closer to the trailers, she noticed most had identification signs on them, which helped. She took the opportunity to give Emily's trailer a once over. One door, just as she thought. Emily had to have known her killer. She would have witnessed the person entering the small trailer. That meant it was either someone associated with the show or possibly a friend. She never mentioned a friend when checking in. Instead, all she did was complain about her ex-husband who she secretly still loved.

"Donna Tollhouse Taber!" a feminine voice called out.

Whoops, she'd lost valuable time speculating on the murderer. At least whoever was signaling her now used her full name. She held up her hand. "Here."

Mona, from the day before, stood in an open trailer doorway attired in the same smock and slacks. A colorful scarf hid most of her hair. It made sense that anyone who had to get up in the middle of the night would have no time to do their own hair and makeup.

Might as well put some zip in her step. She could use all the help she could get, according to clipboard girl. Mona stood waiting without any sign of recognition. Would it be better if she did remember her? The poor woman had to have been in shock and probably didn't remember half of what she said to Donna. It might be best to just wait and see.

"Sorry, I'm late. My husband forgot to tell me I was the new contestant."

Mona made a derisive snort that indicated she didn't entirely buy the story. "Yeah, husbands can be like that. We don't have much time."

No one needed to remind her of that. She trotted up the stairs and waited at the top for Mona to back up and allow her entrance, which she did. Inside, the bright lights around an oversized mirror created illumination that had to be a tad brighter than the sun. No one had to tell Donna to go to the empty chair. She sat, settling her purse in her lap, and peeked into the mirror. "Good heavens! No wonder clipboard girl told me I needed the extra time."

Mona came up behind her, whipped a plastic cape across her shoulders, and tied it in the back. She handed Donna a headband. "Go ahead and put that on. Make sure all your hair around your face is covered—you don't want it to get makeup on it. We don't have time to clean it out."

She took the headband and used it to pull her hair back. "Go ahead and make me beautiful," she joked.

"That depends," Mona said as she stared at a folded piece of paper. "It says here they want a frumpy housewife. I might have to draw in a few more lines."

"What!" Her mouth dropped open in abject horror. "I think I misheard you."

"Nope." Mona shook her head in the mirror, then spun the chair around to face her. "The producer has particular notions about each contestant. One gets to be the glamorous gal, which is obviously not you. Another one is the talented youngster. Only in this case, the woman is in her twenties and my job is to make her look like she's fifteen. Dalton is the male heartthrob. We have an East Indian guy who was actually from Yonkers for the exotic touch. Marjorie is everyone's favorite granny and now, you. The producer wants you to be frumpy."

"I don't want to be frumpy," Donna insisted. Finally, she had an opportunity to be on television and had to intentionally look bad. All those folks who had never met her would think she looked like a house-frau all the time. It wouldn't be good advertisement. There was a reason the more upscale hotels paid for young, sexy couples gazing at each up with absolute devotion as they stayed at the hotel. Ordinary folks either assumed it was where the beautiful people hung out or it encouraged romance. Either way, it was a win-win. No one ever said that when faced with a dumpy female, no matter how good her meatloaf was. Hers was spectacular.

"No worries. Viewers usually like a frumpy character. Gives them a chance to identify with her or feel superior. The downside is the frumpy ones are usually eliminated early, because they are too nice and don't provide enough conflict. We might even have to get a wig for you, too. Some type of graying hair."

Gray hair made her shudder. For years, she'd driven to the next county to have her roots touched up. People assumed she was one of the lucky ones. She didn't spend all that money over the years to prance around in gray hair on television, no less. "If they want conflict, I'll give it to them. Possibly more than they can handle."

Mona chuckled, then sighed. "Thank you. I needed something to cheer me up."

Chapter Ten

DONNA STOOD OUTSIDE the trailer in her gray wig and cotton house dress that made her resemble Mama from the old television show. Mona had explained the producer decided she'd be the grandmotherly sort. When she pointed out they already had a grandmother, Mona smiled. Something was up, besides contestants getting murdered in their trailers. On top of everything, they had the nerve to ask if she would wear a fat suit. They felt she was too thin to be authentic. No, thank you, she had enough padding of her own.

Everything happened so fast, she hadn't even had a chance to check out the local news. What was the local news agency told? The other contestants were waiting inside their air-conditioned trailers waiting for their call. No worries about anyone recognizing her in this get-up. She should have told them she had a stage name. Considering her outfit, it might be something like Grandma Cookie.

Word must have spread there would be another show today. The rented chairs were mostly filled. The crowd wasn't as big as yesterday, probably because people couldn't keep taking days off from work for a show that might not happen. Clipboard girl went out and shushed the audience. A man whom she assumed was the producer came out with a mike today, not a bullhorn, which was much more professional.

"I'm so happy to see all you beautiful people," he said to the audience. The words had the townsfolk grinning and nudging one another. A few probably mentioned the producer looked right at them when he spoke.

"I'm Claude McPherson, the producer of this incredible tribute to the American art of baking."

He made it sound like no one ever put together a pie or baked a loaf of bread before the seventeenth century. Forget about the nursery rhymes concerning pie. They certainly didn't bake in any country other than the good old USA. Comments about the best cooks in the world being in America made Donna smile. Not that she believed it for a minute. Just the other day, she heard ninety percent of Americans use their microwave to cook most foods. Plain puffery to distract from the fact that he was ripping off the British show.

Her nose crinkled as she considered weren't all shows a rip-off of a previous show? Wasn't every game show modeled on some earlier show? Same story with soap operas, which meant the producer really wasn't doing anything everyone had already done.

"As you know, we had a false start yesterday. One of our contestants had a family emergency."

Death usually wasn't her definition of an emergency. It was too late to do anything about it. Did he say her name? It sounded like it. The audience clapped, not the wild clapping you do when your favorite singer takes the stage, but a mild golf tourney clap.

Mona ambled over and stood beside her. "Be ready. He'll say something about each person, then the six of you come out and you're assigned your challenge."

"What's the challenge?"

Mona rolled her eyes. "They're guarding the challenges like it's the formula to Coca Cola. I even heard they locked it in a safe."

It sounded like overkill to Donna. Apparently, they all started at ground zero. It would be something people would consider traditional Americana cooking such as cornpone, biscuits, or apple pie.

The producer had already introduced Harley, a precious child in pigtails and overalls who Mona had disclosed was actually in her twenties. Dalton had been some chef extraordinaire of a restaurant named Paradise Flamingo. She hoped they didn't serve flamingoes. It made her wonder if Emily had once worked in the same restaurant. The producer continued to name contestants. There was a short order cook named Bob and an East Indian named Prashant, who was actually from Yonkers, according to Mona. The only person not mentioned was Marjorie.

Donna wondered what they had done to Marjorie to make her even more grandmotherly. Claude warmed up to his subject, "I know you are going to love this contestant as much as I do. She served as a nurse during the Vietnam War and personally rescued twenty-two soldiers by flying the helicopter after the pilot was wounded."

Really? She flew a helicopter? Those things were difficult to fly, not like a plane that most people could fly easily enough. It was the landing that could prove problematic.

The producer continued. "When she's not busy saving human lives, she works hard to find homes for abandoned pets."

"Please. None of that is true. The woman is staying at my inn." Donna crossed her arms and stared at the producer as he enumerated all the wonderful things Marjorie had done in her life.

"Mrs. Holmes is also a children's author and donates all her profits to Make A Wish Foundation so terminal children can have some fun in their short life."

Did they even bother to research anything? She cut her eyes to

Mona. "Who writes this drivel and a better question is, why? Make a Wish Foundation is a great organization, but they help children with life-threatening diseases, not terminal ones."

"Oh." Mona's eyebrows shot up a little. "I think Tori, the one with the clipboard, wrote that. I think it's too much, myself. No one really likes someone who is too good." She grimaced, then shook her head. "It makes you feel inferior in comparison. I guess they already decided Marjorie as the winner, so they have to make her sound better than the rest." Her hand covered her mouth. "Oops."

"Oops is right." First the indignity of the gray wig, now this. She had half a mind to stalk off the set. If she did, she wouldn't be able to ask any prying questions about Emily.

Mona latched on to her arm. "Please don't tell anyone I told you. Most reality shows are fixed. Surely, you must have guessed that?"

Donna twisted her lips to one side as she considered the possibility. There was that one show where the guy couldn't sing, but he kept progressing. As for those dating shows, maybe people were just that superficial, or it might have been staged. Once she discovered the show was fixed, dozens of possibilities crowded into her head.

"Do the judges know it's fixed?" On her favorite show, they did spend a great deal of time considering the finished product. The one they picked looked superior to the other baked goods.

"Promise me you'll say nothing." Mona still had ahold of Donna's arm.

"I'm not even sure why I'm here with this ridiculous wig on. My original thought was the show wanted someone local who was also a great baker. That's me. Since there's no contest, no glory, nothing matters." It wasn't hard for Donna to look depressed with her unflattering makeup. She might look like she was frowning, even when she wasn't.

"It matters to me." Mona tightened her grip. "You might think it's easy getting a job as a movie makeup artist, but it isn't. There're way too many cosmetologists out there who are tired of doing prom hair and wedding makeup for pennies. Half the time, people don't even tip. They think it's part of the fee. Most probably think they're paying for my time. They have no clue I pay rent on my chair, and I have to buy all my own products, which are only a trifle cheaper than retail, which equals not cheap at all."

Mona took an audible breath while details about the judges were being broadcasted to the audience. She finally dropped her grip and gestured to the trailers. "It may not seem like much to you, but that makeup trailer, this show, is my stair step into a better life. It's pretty obvious the show is being run on a shoestring, but I'm making more than I did at the salon back home. You may not know it, but Atlanta is becoming a cheaper alternative to Hollywood. There've been thirty-odd television shows filmed there. Over 84 important movies have been made there since 2008."

This was news to Donna, and she didn't like being uninformed. "Name one."

"There was a bunch of those Marvel movies like *Thor* and *Spiderman*. You might even remember *The Blind Side*."

She did. "Good movie. So, you want to cash in on all these television shows and movies?"

"I need to. Even though I'm good at what I do, I know the Hollywood market is as glutted with would-be makeup artists as it is starlets. Even if I could get a job, I probably couldn't afford to live there. It also wouldn't be fair to take my kids away from their grandparents. With Dean being dead, I depend on my parents to help with the kids."

"Dean?" Donna repeated the name.

"My husband." Mona swallowed. "He died in an unfortunate accident."

"Oh, I'm sorry." She felt for Mona to be a widow so young. "Car accident?"

"No. Someone shot him. He was a blackjack dealer. A customer thought Dean shafted him and shot him. Security is much better at the casino now." Mona sighed heavily.

Donna could understand a widow who wanted to get ahead and take care of her children. While the story was as mind-numbing as Marjorie's back story, there were holes in it. Georgia had no legalized gambling or casinos. Still, the girl might not be from Georgia. "You live in Atlanta?"

"Mercy, no. I'm a small-town girl. I live in St. Mary's, Georgia."

Before Donna could assure Mona, she'd say nothing, Tori showed up and pointed to the test kitchen where contestants were assembling. "On set. Now."

Someone needed to buy that girl some manners. Donna hustled over to the set faster than her appearance would lead people to expect. There were two judges. A British woman and a bakery guy who was introduced as a pastry chef. The British woman who went by Agatha Fleming clapped her hands together.

"Bakers!" she trilled the word. "Your first challenge is a basic one. Make a classic scone for tea time. You need sixteen perfect ones. You have two hours and the time starts now."

Donna darted into a nearby station while pigtailed Harley asked for a recipe, as did a few others.

Agatha tut-tutted as if it was the silliest thing she'd ever heard. "A scone is a classic. I'm sure you have one in your baking repertoire. If not, the town provides free Internet service. You can look it up on your screen at your station."

The oven was preheating as Donna sifted her flour. *Amateurs.* She tried not to waste time peeking at her competition. A few were pecking away at their keyboards. Good luck with that free service. It was only really good near the base from where it was broadcasted. The closest thing Legacy had to a high rise blocked the signal in one direction, which is why she paid for cable Internet.

Scones were an odd choice for an American show. Not only did they lift the idea from British television, but they also may have taken a few recipes. It would be very telling if the next item they had to make was a meat pasty. Fortunately for Donna, the scone was a time-honored favorite. There were a few things people expected at bed and breakfasts for the morning meal and scones were one of them, along with a specialty coffee. A few expected mimosas and crepes.

Once she rolled the dough, cut the scones in triangles, and put them into the oven, it was icing time. Most people underestimate glaze or icing which really was the most important part of the scone. Without icing, it was little more than a mildly sweet biscuit. There was an ooh from the audience, which caused Donna to look up. A small white floury cloud hung in the air. A flour-covered man let loose with a series of curses. This triggered laughter among the audience and more than a few crew members. The cursing would probably be edited out of the finished show. The only spot not covered in flour was the bald spot on top of his head. From that one clue, she deduced it was Bob, the short order cook.

If she were at home watching the show, she'd assume Bob was clumsy or out of his league. His rushing around frantically caused the mishap, or he purposely did it to lose the challenge while saving face. Knowing what she did, it made her wonder if someone rigged Bob's bag of flour to burst as soon as he lifted it. No time to speculate, she had icing to make. At her station was a cupboard for dry ingredients and a fridge for the perishables. A person was obviously only limited by her ingredients. There were a couple of oranges and a small bottle of maple syrup. It might be a bit more work making her own orange juice, but it should win her points with the judges.

Donna squeezed her eyes shut. Why did she keep forgetting this wasn't a real contest? Still, she owed it to herself to do her best. It would be interesting to see how they could fool the audience. Considering the audience was watching everything each baker did. A man with a camera perched on his shoulder came in closer as she used a grater on the skin of an orange. This resulted in Agatha rushing over to her side.

"I say. What are you up to with the grater?"

It should be obvious what she was up to. Donna looked up at Agatha and smiled. "I'm making orange zest for an orange maple glaze for my scones."

"Brilliant. Can't wait to sample them." Agatha waved at another contestant. "Oh, look, something scrumptious is happening right next door."

The cameraman moved to Harley's station. The girl simpered for the camera as she stirred her mixture. Donna pressed her lips together to prevent anything sarcastic from popping out that might be caught on audio. Good heavens! Was every contestant not only a baker but an aspiring actor, too? She wouldn't be surprised if Harley didn't break into a folksy song to go with her pigtails and overalls. Whatever she was stirring was way too wet to qualify as raw dough. Never mind being scrumptious.

Donna measured her ingredients carefully but listened as Agatha asked Harley what she was working on.

"I decided to go for a raspberry jam filled scone. I prefer a bit of a challenge as opposed to an ordinary scone." Somehow, she managed to keep her down-home accent while implying the rest of them were dullards in the scone department.

A quick glance at the large digital timer placed high above the stations allowed both contestants and the audience to see the elapsed time. Forty-five minutes had ticked off, and Harley hadn't even created anything that was even slightly bread-like. Bob had brushed most of the flour off him but had a late start. Prashant, Marjorie, and Dalton were working away. It appeared as if the trio had their scones in the oven, too.

Agatha and the cameraman wandered over to where Prashant kept an anxious eye on the baking scones. The woman put her hand up to her face and pseudo whispered into the microphone. "Let's see what our nut-brown friend is up to."

Not too surprisingly, Prashant whirled around and glared at the approaching judge. "That was a really racist description. Nut-brown friend? Should I call you my bleached white flour friend? Although, I think *friend* might be a bit too much, since you're British and the oppressor."

"Pardon me?" Agatha tilted her head up, ready to pretend she hadn't heard the baker's words.

"Typical," he muttered and squatted to peer into the glass-fronted oven. "Never willing to take responsibility. Just pretend you didn't take over my country, enslave my people, all in the name of the almighty pound."

Donna assumed that Agatha would let it go. As she recalled there was never any fighting on the British show. Everyone was very earnest. The producer emphasized that this was an American show, which might have been code for lots of conflict. The real question was, was Prashant angry or just playing the part of the angry immigrant?

Agatha's face retained a calmness she may not have felt as Prashant gave his version of the British occupation. Even though the woman came off as uppity, which appeared to be normal for British aristocracy, Donna admired her cool. The woman should be able to run a B and B without blinking an eye.

If none of the contestants knew the show was fixed, each one would do their best to win. That brought her back to Emily. Was she a threat to someone? It sounded extreme. Most murders were personal. Even though parents warn their children about the dangers of strange cities and walking alone, most folks were killed by people they knew. It didn't negate the fact that someone could be robbed in a strange city though.

Behind the oven glass, she saw her scones had turned a perfect golden brown. Donna already had oven mitts on her hands and threw open the door. One second too long and she'd get a pitying look from the bakery guy. If he was anything like his English counterpart, he would pretend sympathy, while mentioning everything that was wrong with the pastry.

Seventeen perfect golden-brown triangles were carefully moved to the cooling rack. Donna made an extra one she could sample. It would help her determine how fixed this contest really was. On one hand, Mona could be making this up as she went along. Lots of people did that. She even knew one or two. It made them feel important.

She packed her icing into a decorating bag with a small circular tip that would create a nice line. Originally, she was going with a glaze but decided she needed more oomph. Fancy always won over plain, especially if fancy was yummy, too.

Once the scones were decorated, she arranged them on a cake stand that she draped a floral napkin over. *Perfect.* She might as well nibble on the sample one.

Chapter Eleven

THE OTHER BAKERS rushed around as the commentator encouraged the audience to count down with him. It reminded Donna of the crowds on various New Year's Eve shows, although this crowd wasn't bundled up against the chill. If the contestants thought they might be offered their own cooking show, the citizens of Legacy must have had somewhat similar thoughts judging by the Sunday Best on display in the audience, along with the Easter hats. She imagined whoever sat behind the hat-wearing women would be miffed. They would have no chance of seeing anything.

Donna relaxed against the counter, enjoying watching the frantic actions of her competitors. Knowing a recipe had saved her time. Harley poked at scones that didn't quite look done and appeared to be bleeding—not exactly scrumptious. It would be interesting to see who would win this round and who would go home. It might let her know if the show was fake or real.

The loud buzzer caused Marjorie to be startled and drop a platter of lovely scones. It shattered on the hard floor, causing the audience to make sympathetic murmurs. There went another competitor. Donna did a slow survey of the glammed-up Marjorie from her high heels to her single string of pearls. The cashmere twin set had to be too hot for the kitchen, and it must be challenging to bend in the pencil skirt. There had to be someone on staff who remembered Donna Reed, judging by Marjorie's outfit. The running joke was Donna Reed vacuumed in high heels and pearls, so why couldn't all women of that time do likewise?

It was so obvious that Marjorie was meant to be the winner from her heart-wrenching bio to her much-improved appearance. The woman had a waistline, which wasn't there when she checked in. Maybe Mona could tell her what brand of shapewear she was wearing.

The emcee of the contest reappeared and waved at the audience as he took center stage. "Alrighty, ladies and gentlemen, the moment we've been waiting for is here. Let's give our hard-working contestants a big round of applause."

The audience clapped on cue, and there were a few whistles.

"Way to go, Donna!" someone shouted.

She had a fan! The prospect had her pushing her shoulders back and searching the sea of fancy hats for a familiar face. With the hats casting shadows on both the wearer and those nearby, it was hard to tell who was who.

The pastry chef judge reappeared and waved at the audience, making Donna wonder where he had been while Agatha made small talk with all the contestants. Maybe he wasn't paid enough to be on camera for very long. It could also be that he didn't perform well, not being an actual actor.

The emcee turned to the pastry guy as if they were old friends. "Welcome back, Mason."

In case the audience had somehow forgotten in the two hours that Mason had been gone, his baking history was repeated as the man shifted his weight from one foot to another.

Not an actor. Donna kept the judgment to herself but might share it with Mark later. Agatha joined the emcee and pastry chef, giving the emcee a frosty smile. What was up with that?

"Your mission," the emcee stated with an air of gravity as if he were addressing future astronauts, "was to make sixteen perfect scones suitable for breakfast or a tea party."

The audience broke into chatter as if this had been a surprise to them. It shouldn't be. More likely people were sharing their predictions about who would win. Money possibly might change hands when the winner was announced.

He strolled across the test kitchen, waiting for the chatter to die down. He stopped right in front of Donna's station, giving her time to assess his wide shoulders. He was big enough, Donna concluded, to snap Emily's neck like a twig. Still, the man was in a suit of what she referred to as *early summer*, although most people insisted on calling it *spring*. Suits hid a lot. They were the push-up bra of the masculine set. It was a safe bet that the man discarded those wide shoulders before he left for the day.

Acting wasn't associated with muscles, unless someone was an action hero type, always ripping off his shirt for a scene. It might have been easier since Emily was seated. Besides the element of surprise, all even a smaller man would have to do was use his weight and twist. The thought made her shudder.

The emcee spoke. "Nervous?" Then held the mic in front of Donna.

"No, I made a scone that is a favorite of my guests…"

One of the crew members gestured to the emcee. "Need you up front."

The mic vanished before she even got to name her inn. So far, the free publicity hadn't made an appearance.

Mason and Agatha strolled to each station commenting on the finished product. First up was Bob, who still had a dusting of flour on his hair and a speck on his nose.

Mason was the first to speak. "I heard you had a mishap. I wasn't here to see. Why don't we replay it on the monitors?"

Heads turned toward the screens as everyone watched except Bob. There were a few titters, less than before. Donna was glad of that. She didn't want the rest of the country to consider the Legacy community as a hotbed of mean-spiritedness. That would do nothing for tourism.

After the clip played, Mason turned toward Bob. "Any scones?"

"Not yet," Bob indicated the oven. "I have chocolate chip ones in the oven. It will only be a few more minutes."

Agatha pursed her lips, then said, "What a shame. You know the rules. The product has to be completed within the time you've been given."

"Yes," Bob agreed and hung his head.

Even though he was her competitor, Donna experienced sympathy for the man who might just be an unknowing dupe. Naturally, she assumed the show had decided ahead of time who would go out and set up the station for things not to go well. What if it was another competitor? She knew it wasn't her or Bob, so that left four people.

The show's favorite, Marjorie, lost her place in the running. None of the judges would touch scones that had kissed the floor. They moved on next to Harley and her bleeding travesty of a scone. Agatha nudged Mason and pointed to the scones. The pastry chef picked up one as the filling oozed down his arm.

While Mason grimaced, Agatha talked. "Oh my, something didn't go right here. You weren't planning on giving us both salmonella with your under baked scone?"

"I wouldn't do that!" Harley insisted with rounded eyes and a determined set to her chin.

Agatha cut her eyes to Mason, who held up the offending scone. A light mutter broke out among the audience, but it didn't stop Agatha from talking.

"Yes, you would have with that scone. Fortunately, we're both too smart to eat it."

The duo moved on to rip the heart out of another contestant. They stopped at Dalton's station and pronounced his scone to be overbaked and dry. Then it was on to Prashant's cleverly decorated scone. He had iced them green and used tiny flower candies on top of them. They did look good. Prashant could win—this round.

Agatha surveyed the scone and made a moue of distaste. "This is a Christmas cookie, not a scone. Are you familiar with what a scone is?"

Donna inhaled deeply, wondering how Prashant would handle that. Mason bit into the scone and declared, "Delicious."

This forced Agatha to do likewise. She chewed while somehow maintaining a sour expression. "It's acceptable. Those tiny flowers grate on my teeth. Where did you get those from?"

Even from this distance, she could see Prashant's clenched jaw and folded arms. "I brought them with me."

Agatha stumbled back a step as if he had mentioned he carried a vial of smallpox and was about to empty it onto his station, infecting everyone within a thousand feet. She pressed her hand to her lips. Mason rushed over to her and put his hand under her elbow as if she would faint.

The judge pulled herself together and gave a disdainful sniff. "Oh, that won't do. It won't do at all. Contestants are not allowed to bring in their own decorations."

"No one mentioned this," Prashant pointed out.

Before Agatha could say anything else, Donna spoke. "It wasn't.

I listened closely." She cupped her hands around her mouth and directed her comment to the audience. "Did anyone hear the emcee say you couldn't bring your own decorations?"

Most yelled back, "No!"

A handful yelled "What?"

One joker answered with "That's what she said!"

Instead of correcting her mistake, Agatha motioned in Donna's direction, and the two made the half-dozen steps to her station. The cameraman zoomed in on the plate of artfully arranged scones. "I say, this is superior," Agatha crooned while Mason picked up one and bit into it.

"Yummy. It melts in my mouth. It has just the right amount of crumbliness and sweetness. I can see eating this with some jam and clotted cream."

Despite Mason's high praise, Agatha acted skeptical and picked up a scone, sniffed it, then took the tiniest bite, then another. "It *is* good." She said the words as if they came as a surprise to her.

Donna smiled. It always made her happy when someone enjoyed her cooking. Day one ended with Bob being told goodbye, despite his chocolate chip scones being amazing. He hadn't set up his station, so he shouldn't bear the blame. For reasons unknown to Donna, there was definite conflict between Agatha and Prashant, unless they were supposed to play it that way.

When they announced her name as the winner, Donna didn't react immediately. Instead, she was carefully eyeing crew members who danced around the edges of the test kitchen in a highly orchestrated dance. Prashant came over and shook her shoulder. "You won this round. Go forward for pictures and stuff."

She won? There would be pictures? Good heavens! No way was she going to be photographed in this horrendous get-up. "Just a minute," she trilled, then ducked down behind her station. The oven door worked as a mirror as she pulled off the wig and finger combed her hair. A wet dishrag removed most of her grayish makeup that aged her. She attacked it so vigorously with the washcloth that her cheeks were rosy. "Ready," she popped up and joined the emcee and judges.

Mason, who must be the comic relief in the duo, acted stunned. "What did you do with Donna?"

"Here I am, the owner of The Painted Lady Inn, where you're guaranteed award-winning scones await you for breakfast." At last! She had finally got in the name of her inn.

The producer shook his head. "We ran over on time. We may cut that last bit out."

"Cut it out?" It was partially the reason she was here. "Why not cut out Bob being covered with flour for the second time out? Showing it twice when you asked Bob to leave will play as being a bit of a bully."

The producer scratched his head and ambled away as if he hadn't heard a word she said. "That's a wrap!" he yelled to the rest of the crew.

Chapter Twelve

ONCE THE PRODUCER announced the show was done for the day, murmuring voices grew louder as crew people swarmed the test kitchen. Donna backed up against a counter, unsure of what she was supposed to do.

"Donna Tollhouse Tabber!"

The sound of her name being mispronounced had Donna pivoting to see who was mangling it. Tori, better known as Clipboard Girl, nodded as she strolled closer and spoke.

"Claude really liked the reveal thing you did at the end. He's sure viewers will tune in to see what else you might do." Her lips pulled up into what some might call a smile, others might label it an expression of pain. "Lucky you."

The woman moved on, not even giving Donna a chance to reply. It obviously wasn't a conversation as she originally thought. The remark *lucky you* normally would be a congratulations of sorts. Sometimes it was used to point out that whatever the person had done had no merit and somehow got noticed, which made the individual lucky. Somehow, she thought Tori meant the latter. It hadn't escaped Donna's notice that Clipboard Girl made a point of using the producer's first name as if they were buddies. It's possible they were friends, but it was more likely Tori wanted her to think that.

With the day's shooting over, the crew hustled around removing all the electronic equipment that would be ruined by the salt-tinged coastal air. So far, they had avoided the pop-up showers, too. Although England probably had more rain days per year than Legacy, it made her wonder why every show featured a beautiful sunny day complete with flowers and baby farm animals in the opening scenes. If they wanted animals for their opening shots, probably the best Legacy could offer was a close-up of the crabs scuttling away from the gulls. It didn't have the same appeal as baby lambs.

Even though she was not a fan of it, the gray wig cost money. She needed to return it to the makeup trailer. They might even try to bill her for it or dock her pay. Did people get paid for this? One of her retired cousins appeared regularly as an extra in the various shows and movies being staged in Atlanta. Whenever there was a call for an old white lady, she was there. At best, she made seventy dollars a day for walking across a street or appearing in a crowd. Sometimes her two seconds of celluloid fame ended up on the editing room floor. Still, she had a bit more to talk about when she met the other retired teachers for coffee.

Everyone appeared to have a task and rushed to get it done. Cords were rolled up while lights were covered with tarp. The sucking sound of a vacuum meant someone had the unwelcome job of cleaning up the flour fiasco. A squeak of a cart caught her attention as another employee followed the sweeper person, removing all the ingredients from each station.

The wig momentarily forgotten, she dashed over to the person who was picking up supplies, counting them, and tallying her inventory. "Hello. I see you're picking up ingredients."

"That's my job," replied the older man who barely reached Donna's chin, which should put him around five-foot-four.

"Did you put out the supplies, too?" She hoped she asked in a casual enough voice. His narrowed eyes said otherwise as his brows met.

"You're saying did I screw with the flour to make it go all over that poor guy?" He shook his head. "I actually liked Bob. Maybe was even rooting for him a little. His bag of flour was the same as the rest." He held up a hand. "You can't pin that on me. It's possible someone else could have screwed with it." His shoulders went up in a shrug. "Don't know who. Still, Claude didn't spring for security. Felt that in a small town he wouldn't need it. A cheap SOB, that's what he is. Anyone could have tampered with it. Even some locals who thought it might provide a good laugh." He sighed. "Poor Bob."

"I feel for him, too. His chocolate chip scones were quite nice when they were finally done," Donna added, hoping to strike a sympathetic note.

"Probably better than yours," the man snapped.

Well, she wouldn't go that far. Still, she worked to maintain an emotionless visage like Agatha. It would be hard to know if she was succeeding without a mirror. "Is that why you have to pack up all the ingredients?"

"Not the original reason," he paused and gave her a suspicious look. "Why do you want to know?"

Sometimes, the truth disarmed people. "I'm nosy. Always have been all my life."

"You are, that's for sure." He managed a raspy chuckle. "Two reasons. The bugs here are large enough to pick up a car. I wouldn't be surprised if they could open a fridge or cabinet door. The second reason is our cheap producer has all the ingredients carefully measured out. We should have just enough for all the recipes, not a teaspoon more."

"Good to know," Donna murmured more to herself as she mentally reviewed the extra flour, she had used to make the extra scone. Would it ruin her chances?

The man's shaggy brows lifted. "Hey, aren't you one of the bakers? Trying to get some secret information?"

Well, actually she was. Not the type of information he thought, though. "Do you have any?"

"No."

She shrugged. "Then how could I get any?"

This caused a raspy laugh that morphed into a cough. When he finally got his breath back, he gave Donna a crooked smile. "I like you. If I can root for Bob, I guess I can root for you. What's your name, girlie?"

Even though she knew he was talking to her, Donna made a pretense of looking behind her. "I don't see any girlie, here. My name's Donna Tollhouse Taber."

"Set me back, didn't you? I'll remember you." His eyes twinkled, then he added, "Girlie."

So, he was going to play that game. "See you around, *boy.*" As she strolled away, she could hear his hoarse laughter. Two things had come out of their conversation, or make that three. The flour bag had been fine when placed in the cabinet. There was no security to track any unauthorized folks on the set. If it cost extra, it wasn't happening. Claude was cheap. The most obvious thing she learned was the one not stated. No one mentioned Emily had been killed.

She knew because Mark knew. While she saw the paramedics show up, she didn't see them leave. A black body bag strapped to the gurney would certainly tell a story. What if no one had seen one? Maybe Claude had managed to swear the few who knew to secrecy. Her exhausted husband hardly spoke more than a handful of words when he arrived home the night before. Even the exciting prospect of her being a contestant was never mentioned until the phone rang this morning. What if the producer thought he was buying Mark's silence by allowing his wife to participate?

Her husband wouldn't take a bribe. That was one thing she was sure of. It might not even have the appearance to Mark. Once Claude discovered his contestant was dead and Mark stood beside him watching the medical examiner examine the body, he might have asked if he knew someone who wanted to be a contestant. Any good husband would have suggested his own wife, certain she was the best cook in the world, however, more and more women were getting by with prepared meals or even picking up dinner through a drive-thru. There may not have been as many eager potential contestants as she originally thought. Anyhow, the medical examiner and Mark wouldn't have said anything. In her experience, her close-mouthed husband never leaked information that only the murderer would know. Often, that is how the murderer was apprehended.

The makeup trailer had the door propped open. Not exactly secure, considering how expensive makeup and wigs were. No one was inside. Her intention was to leave the wig but not without a note. There were no handy sticky notes, so she resorted to the back of a receipt to scribble her note. Knowing how things could get misplaced, she felt for her phone, which she had slipped into her pocket. The man in charge of supplies was right. There was no security.

Using her phone, she snapped a photo of her note. Curiosity prompted her to turn the note over only to discover it was for baby wipes, paper towels, and latex gloves. A killer might use latex gloves, but if he actually bought them, he wouldn't be stupid enough to leave the receipt laying around. Then again, dumber criminals *had* been apprehended. Donna grabbed the receipt by the edge and slid it into her pocket. There might be some worthwhile prints on it, besides her own.

That left her with finding another piece of paper to leave a note on. She scrounged around, not finding anything. When she decided to try her luck with the waste can, which had to be a germ haven, she heard footsteps on the stairs.

"What are you doing here?"

Donna spun to watch Mona enter the trailer. Her unsmiling face and tense body language spoke volumes about her state of being, especially combined with her growled words.

"I was returning the wig and wanted to write you a note, but I couldn't find anything to write one on."

"Fine. You brought the wig back. Word is you won't be wearing it anymore. I guess it's going to be the Glamorous Grandma show now." She grabbed the wig and threw it in a bin.

"Ah, thank you. What time should I be back tomorrow?" It would be nice for a change not to be propelled out of bed by a phone call.

"Six-thirty on the dot. Didn't you read your instructions sheet? Everyone around here is such a diva," she grumbled the words as she capped the makeup left on the vanity.

Donna paused, already disturbed by the notion of everyone calling her a grandmother. Technically at her age, she could be a very *young* grandmother. Not Loretta Lynn young, but still not old enough to be a conventional nana. She knew she was lying to herself, but it was one she wanted to believe. As for the instruction sheet, she had received none. Good chance there was a folded one in the pants Mark wore last night. "See you then."

The woman grunted, not a bit like her earlier self. Show business people. Who could figure them out? Donna left, anxious to get back to the world she knew. Her phone vibrated in her pocket, but she delayed looking at it until she'd obtained her purse and was in her car.

It was a message from her mother. *I'm safe. Don't worry.*

Really? That was the message? Donna typed away, firing questions. *Where are you? What are you doing? Is Simon with you? When will you be back?*

A reply came back almost immediately. *That's for me to know and you to find out. LOL.*

Was this a test of her fact-finding skills? If so, her mother had picked a bad time. Maybe Maria received a more informative message, not being a relative and all. Tapping on her car window stopped Donna from starting the engine. Janice's flaming red hair identified her friend more than anything. A finger tap had the window descending. Janice was the first to speak.

"Whoa. Look at you, television star. I wouldn't mind being on the show, but I'm not sure any other contestants would conveniently have a family emergency." She wrinkled her nose at the possibility.

Not thinking, Donna opened her mouth to tell Janice that there was no family emergency. If no one was talking, maybe she shouldn't, even if there was no way Janice was a killer. Still, she understood a secret was best kept if one of the people told was dead. To protect her friend, she'd say nothing. That way her friend wouldn't *accidentally* share the info and make it possible to soon be common knowledge.

"I doubt that will happen, but it can't hurt to tell the producer of your interest." She didn't think another contestant would bow out, but on the other hand, she didn't want to disappoint her friend, either.

"I already did." She winced slightly. "Truthfully, I only got as far as some chick carrying a clipboard, but she *did* take my business card."

Who needs security, when they had Tori? "Ah, yes, Tori. She's good friends with the producer."

Janice's eyebrows lifted. "Yes, I know. She told me she and Claude were good friends. I think those two might be knocking boots."

"I think that's what she wants people to think." Donna reflected back on all that she'd seen that morning. "I never saw those two exchange a word or even stand close to each other."

"Makes sense," Janice nodded, then reached into the car and slapped Donna on the back. "You're the lucky one. Enjoy."

There were those words again, *lucky one*. At least she knew her friend meant it in the best way. "Yes, I am. It's not at all like the show, but I'm dealing with it."

Janice's phone chimed. Her friend stared at a text and frowned. "Another produce emergency. I swear, every time I leave the restaurant, everything goes to H E double hockey sticks. Gotta run." She waved and speed walked away to wherever her vehicle was parked.

Too bad about the produce disaster. At least she didn't have a similar issue to go home to. Who knows how Mark handled the breakfast crowd? They had a drawer of breakfast vouchers for Kasey Lynn's Country Kitchen for when emergencies hit. Kasey took the vouchers, then billed the inn. Donna tried to not use the vouchers, considering she had food in her pantry. Oh well, she'd deal with it, along with her runaway mother, who was fine, and with any luck, Ten would not want to talk to her about his love life.

Chapter Thirteen

AN ACRID ODOR of something burning hit Donna as she opened the back door of the inn. "Hell's Bells!" She dashed into the narrow hallway, trying to remember where she put the fire extinguisher. Law required that no one should walk more than seventy-five feet to reach a fire extinguisher. With any luck, Mark replaced the extinguisher after he put out a guest's car fire. She darted into the hall closet where she had stowed one of the extinguishers. Nothing.

There was another in the kitchen. That's where most fires started. What about the guests? Should she evacuate the place? It might be better to see what the smell was first. Her nostrils vibrated as she pulled in the scent. Hot metal, cast iron to be exact, which caused her alarm to dissipate a little. Meat, along with onions, possibly mushrooms. She identified the smells as she entered the kitchen. Her favorite cast iron skillet sat smoking on the stove top.

"Good gravy!" She ran toward the stove and used the hem of her shirt wrapped around her hand to pull the skillet off the stove. "Ouch!" As hot pads went, it hadn't worked too well. Donna switched on the vent fan and surveyed the kitchen. Open spices sat by the stove along with a half cake of semi-melted Irish butter. There were a couple of dirty dishes on the counter along with serving spoons. One of her much-used cookbooks sat open on the counter.

Had the guests started cooking for themselves? The fridge came equipped with a lock she used most of the time. The freezer and wine she kept locked up in the basement. Donna ran to the basement door only to find the padlock hanging open. Where was Ten? Surely Mark had him handle everything. Instead of looking for her helper, Donna stood in place and yelled. "Ten! Ten! Where are you?"

The lanky soon-to-be college graduate jogged into view. "Shhhh." He held his finger to his lips. "I'm making my grand gesture like your mother suggested."

"Grand gesture?" Donna exhaled, wondering what craziness could be laid at her mother's feet. Her mother favored the flamboyant, while Donna was more of the practical sort.

"Yes." Ten kept his voice low and angled his head to the side, indicating the dining room. "I made Sloane a romantic lunch. It should have been dinner, but I couldn't guarantee most of the guests would be gone by then. Besides, babes love men who can cook."

Donna rolled her eyes and pointed to herself. "This babe appreciates men who clean up after themselves."

"I will," he promised. "I need to return to Sloane. It's a wasted grand gesture if I'm not there."

"True." She gestured to the open padlock. "You?"

"Ah, yes. I needed the Yakima Valley Cabernet to pair with the steak." He reached past Donna and closed the padlock, securing the basement. He pivoted and returned to the dining room.

Donna watched him go with a sense of quiet pride. She might not have taught the boy much, but he could pick a decent wine to go with steak, which she had identified by its scent. He also used a cookbook, another plus. She sighed, then put on an apron. Sure, she should let him clean the kitchen himself, but soon enough he'd be gone. There'd be no helping himself to food or wine that she intended for elsewhere. Nor would there be stories of love lost. She would miss him. It wouldn't hurt her to clean up one of his messes as he tried to patch together his romance. *Young love.* It made her shake her head. Everything was so dramatic.

She moved to the sink and filled it with soapy water as her thoughts drifted to Emily. As a young person, she could be dramatic. The young tended to think everything was a matter of life and death. Of course, for Emily, it was.

Donna moved around the room picking up dirty dishes and carrying them back to the sink. Cleaning helped center her thoughts, rather like cooking. So far, she knew Emily loved her ex-husband, which in itself was odd. Whoever came into the trailer, she knew. It must have been someone who didn't frighten her. She was still in her chair, although the murderer could have carried her to the chair and posed the body.

As she washed each dish and utensil, she considered who could want to kill Emily. Was she a really good chef? Someone might consider her as too much competition. It would bear looking into. First, she could look up Dalton's restaurant on social media. While they may have updated the website, she could probably find an old reference in the review section if Emily was a chef. The reviewers often fancied themselves professionals and went into detail about a dish and often mentioned the chef by name as if they were old school buddies.

Once she rinsed, dried, and put away the dishes, she was ready to salvage the cast iron skillet. The memory of herself sending Emily's personal journal to her own email returned. It made her wonder if the police had been here yet. Mark understood the need to keep things low-key. It would never do to have police trooping up and down the staircase. Did Dalton even know? Better yet, was

Dalton the killer? It would help to know why the two divorced. How in the world would she casually introduce *that* into a conversation?

Once done with the dishes, she tiptoed past the dining room, resisted the urge to peek, and hurried down the hall to use the elevator. In the interest of health, she used the stairs as much as possible. Even though it was only one o'clock, it felt as if she'd been working all day. The elevator made a noisy ascent. It was one of the more inexpensive models. No one would sneak up to any floor using it. It shuddered to a stop on the third floor.

No sound of televisions or muted conversations came from any of the rooms. Everyone must have left. The question was, did they leave before the police arrived or after? She assumed Mark or Ten passed out the meal vouchers. Once the people had left the inn in search of breakfast, they probably stayed gone, investigating Legacy's wealth of quirky boutiques and antique shops. They might have even headed out to the beach, which is one of the main reasons people vacationed in Legacy.

Donna moved toward Emily's room and noticed a slash of yellow. Unlike the yellow ribbons in the song meaning it was okay to come home, this ribbon meant the police had closed the room. It wasn't too noticeable. She appreciated the consideration. It may have helped that she had the detective investigating the case living at the inn. It was a two-way street, which meant no opening the door until she was told to.

The police had probably gathered up all Emily's belongings to paw through at the station. Somehow, Donna felt the deceased guest would be appalled at strangers holding up her underwear and speculating about what type of person she was. It was always like that when a murder happened. All the speculation about who the person was and a possible hidden life.

Thank goodness she took photos and emailed the document to herself. She moved past the doors, noticing the maid service requests. Geesh, didn't the guests know she had a crime to solve? With any luck, Sloane would be gone when she reached the second floor, which would allow Ten to help.

Donna gathered up her cleaning equipment and moved to the first room. She opened up the door and sighed. "Someone had a good time."

Food carry-out containers and beverage cans littered the surfaces. Clothes were strewn about as if a two-year-old had opened the suitcase and threw out garments in gleeful abandon.

"Good heavens. It looks like they lived here for a month as opposed to a day or so."

Donna pulled on her rubber gloves. Most people hated to clean bathrooms, and she wasn't a fan, but the clothes were the worst. Guests could freak out at the thought of someone touching their clothes. Still, it was impossible to sweep or make up a bed when clothes were everywhere. All she could do was pick them up and drape them over a chair. Unfortunately, she could be mingling the dirty with the clean. Still, if the guest wanted otherwise, they could have kept them in their suitcase or hung them up in the wardrobe.

It took her a little longer to clean the third floor than she expected, but Ten joined her on the second, and they worked together. His happy attitude told the tale, but she chose to ask anyhow. "How did lunch go?"

"Perfect. I think that's what we needed, more us time."

"Makes sense," Donna agreed, while she thought otherwise. As young people, they had plenty of *us* time. As harried professionals, they'd soon discover that *us* time often occurred at the end of the day, usually between dinner and sleep. If they were lucky, they could catch up on the weekend between errands. "You talk to any of the guests?"

"You mean besides saying have a nice breakfast as I handed them a meal voucher?" Ten commented as he picked up an armload of white bath towels.

"Yes." Donna glanced at the interior of the linen closet. "We'll need to do laundry today. We're almost out of towels." She'd heard that some B and B owners made guests use the same towels over and over by stating it was for the environment. Most of her guests must not have cared about the environment. They wanted fresh towels every day. A few wanted them twice a day. It was Ten's job to handle the inn laundry.

Instead of him grimacing as he would have done before, Ten laughed. "That means I have laundry to do. No problem. That's the least I can do considering I used your food and wine. You even cleaned up the kitchen for me. Thank you."

"It's the least I can do to help out with your grand gesture. Have you heard from my mother?"

He shook his head. "No. You?"

"In a way. She sent me a text saying she was fine."

"That's good, right?" He grabbed a cleaning caddy with his other hand.

"Yes. I guess I wonder what she's up to. You know Cecilia. It's probably something adventurous. As her only daughter, I feel left out."

Ten put down the caddy to pat her arm. "Sometimes, if you love someone you have to set them free."

Donna inhaled deeply, trying not to show how his remark amused her. Here, her young employee was quoting from a book that was popular in the seventies before he was even born. "I'll keep that in mind."

By four, Ten was working on the laundry while Donna booted up the computer. The Paradise Flamingo website featured two pink flamingoes with their necks intertwined. At the top was a banner, including links to a menu and reviews. Curious, Donna clicked on the menu to see what trademark dish entry snagged Dalton as a contestant.

The dishes all had colorful names such as *Tropical Delight, Sail Away Shrimp*, and *Beach Barbeque*. Each item had a detailed description. It was, at best, a little more than bar food with a heavy emphasis on seafood. Weird.

Maybe they had amazing desserts. Donna scrolled down the menu to find *Key Lime Pie*, ice cream sundaes, and a *Parrot Parfait*, which she sincerely hoped did not include any part of the colorful bird. It couldn't be the desserts. What, then?

The reviews bragged about excellent macaroni and cheese, which most anyone could make. Many remarked on great service and a fun atmosphere. Although there were mainly positive reviews, some were not so pleasant. They complained of shrimp so small that you would need a magnifying glass to see it. Others commented about over salted food and watered-down drinks.

Even if Dalton had entered the contest, there was no way he should have beat out so many other entries. It made her wonder if there was even a contest. There was an *about us* label she decided to click on. She might as well see what was what. A click revealed a photo of a smiling Emily and Dalton. He had his arm around her, and they looked happy. Websites masters could be expensive, but she would have thought divorced folks would have sprung to get an update to their site. Dalton was listed as a pastry chef, while Emily's mini-bio listed her as a business major and sous chef. No way would a pastry chef and a sous chef serve the entrees that passed for food at the Flamingo. Her lips twisted as she considered the conundrum, then she snorted. How could she have forgotten the most basic fact that being an amateur sleuth taught her?

People lie. They lied about little things such as their age, their income, their weight, or natural hair color. Many chose to pad out their resumes by giving themselves awards they never received or graduating from Ivy League schools. It wouldn't be a far stretch for Emily and Dalton to give themselves titles they didn't deserve.

It made her wonder why they did it. Their customers weren't ones who searched out restaurants that had Cordon Bleu trained chefs. So far, nothing made sense. Donna decided to move on to the journal.

The email document opened without any trouble. Guilt poked at her. Necessity had her digging through someone's personal journal. She should have told Mark. Forensic computer experts could unearth it, along with whatever was on the laptop.

The beginning of the document started with Emily gushing about their good fortune. She couldn't believe they were approached by talent scouts for a television show. Both she and Dalton would be on a type of reality show. The scouts had promised all they had to do was be themselves and be photogenic. They were both good looking, so they had that covered.

There were no applications to be on the show. It made Donna wonder who the talent scouts were and what were the requirements to be a contestant? Even though she considered herself an accomplished cook, there was no way the producer knew that. Mark could just be another husband bragging on his wife's cooking.

So far, Dalton and Emily were married. It made her wonder why the woman decided to start journaling. Did she think something was up? Maybe she thought the show would make her into such a big celebrity that she'd be writing a tell-all book.

Her phone chimed. She pulled it out of her pocket and answered it. "Hello, Kathy. What's up? You do remember I retired from the hospital?"

Her friend chuckled before answering, "I do. That's why I called. I know you miss out on hospital gossip."

Her brows beetled together, trying to imagine what tidbit had her former colleague calling. She didn't care what nurse or doctor were making cow eyes at each other. "What's the story?"

"Congratulations! I hear you're on that baking show they're filming, right?"

"That, I am." It didn't surprise her that the news of her television debut had reached her former workplace. The image of Kathy dressed in her scrubs, possibly hiding out in the breakroom to make the call brought back memories. It hadn't been that long since she officially retired—only months—but sometimes it felt more like years.

"That was always your dream, wasn't it?"

The question made Donna pause for a few seconds. Owning the inn had been her dream, which she'd accomplished. Turning it into a bed and breakfast checked another item off her list. Even solving murders with her now husband had also been part of that dream. Not that she would ever admit that to anyone. It would just make her sound morbid. "No, it wasn't a dream, but I thought it might be fun, rather like a vacation. My life can't be hospital gossip."

"Not today, anyhow. Many of us are envious you got to throw away the crepe sole nursing shoes. It must be nice to be retired."

"Please." She felt the need to correct her former co-worker. Too many people assumed she now had a blissful life where she slept in and greeted a few guests when they arrived. They were unaware that instead of scrubbing one toilet, she did nine, as well as making up numerous beds. "I may be busier now than when I was simply a nurse."

Donna didn't bother to mention the fact that when Mark entered her life, it became increasingly more complicated. Not from the romance angle, although there was that, but more from the help, often unasked for, that she gave to the various crimes her sweetie endeavored to solve.

"Yeah, yeah. Cry me a river. We all know you have the good life. Still, being on the baking show and all, I had news that might impact your future career as a television chef. One of the judges…" she began, but Donna interrupted.

"Which one?"

"Oh, the snotty British one. Although, the way she was cursing when they brought her in had me doubting her accent a wee bit myself."

Maria may have said something similar about the woman, too. "Why was she in the hospital?"

"Poisoning."

Her first thought, while not being sympathetic, was practical. At least she hadn't stayed at the inn, which meant the poisoning couldn't be pinned on her. The image of Agatha enunciating the words *our nut-brown friend* in her superior way came to mind. "Type of poison?"

"Arsenic."

It was a common enough poison that anyone could get their hands on. It was usually used to kill rats. Still, it usually took a build-up of small amounts to kill a person. It didn't mean the poisoner knew that. At least Agatha was smart enough to go to the hospital.

Well, there went Donna's shot at show biz.

Chapter Fourteen

W HO WOULD WANT to poison Agatha? The better question might be who wouldn't? This would take some real thought. After saying goodbye to her friend, she went into the front parlor and sat in her favorite wing chair, the one with a floral chintz cover and angled slightly toward the fireplace. Legacy squatted on the edge of South Carolina with a climate that didn't require a wood fire. It didn't stop Donna from building one in the colder months. Not only did she enjoy flames, but they gave the inn a cozy feel. Instead of a fire or even logs, Maria had put metal candle holders of different sizes, with the tallest being in the middle. When lit, they provided the same coziness without the heat.

Now they were unlit, no light to enliven the fireplace or apparently Donna's imagination as she stared at the candlesticks.

Agatha was a little over the top, rather like an acerbic relative—who always had a dig for everyone—people endured due to her age or they only saw a few times a year. There could be the possibility of being cut out of the will, too. Only with the show, it would be early elimination as opposed to a will.

She sighed heavily in the stillness of the inn. Eliminating a judge was no recipe for winning. Her mind immediately went to Prashant and how reactive he had been to Agatha. Whatever she said, he took as an insult while her intention may not have been meant as such. Then again, maybe it was. Mona, the makeup artist, had mentioned something about conflict being important. Or was it drama? They were both pretty much the same.

It was hard to know how anyone truly felt. She wasn't sure who was acting and who was being real. Obviously, Harley, in her country-girl disguise was acting. Maybe Agatha was, too. Judging by Emily's journal, she'd been putting on a front. Was it because of the show or could it have been how she suddenly had to work with her ex-husband? For all Donna knew, Dalton could have married one of his restaurant employees or his girlfriend on the side. As a woman, she assumed naturally that Dalton was at fault, but Emily mentioned divorcing Dalton had been the biggest mistake of her life. That made it sound like she'd had control over the outcome. The fact that she still loved him was the most puzzling.

What had Dalton done that Emily felt was unforgivable or, at least, it was at the time? The clock on the mantle ticked loudly, reminding her that time was passing. Most police officers knew murderers were best caught in forty-eight hours after committing the crime. That's when the evidence was the freshest and the murder was uppermost in everyone's minds. Those who may have seen something would come forward, especially if money was offered for a credible tip.

Twenty-four hours had passed since Emily's sudden departure from this life. The entire show and crew could disappear with Agatha's poisoning. Along with it would go the murderer—not if she could help it, though. She blew out a slow breath. Her brother might question why she thought the murderer had something to do with the show. Daniel might be good at construction, but he missed the obvious when it came to solving crimes.

Unless it was a total random shooting like a drive-by, there was a reason an individual was killed. A drive-by, a bombing... Those acts of violence were meant to take out as many people as possible, and it didn't matter who it was. In solitary murders, the victim usually knew their killer, which made it personal, especially when robbery wasn't involved. No one in Legacy knew any of the baking show folks. There'd be no reason for the locals to resort to murder. As for Emily's ex, they were already divorced. Most men intent on murder made sure to kill their wives before the divorce was final.

Her phone chimed, drawing her from her musing. A quick peek revealed a text from her mother. *You and Mark are invited to Simon and my wedding at six tonight in Las Vegas.*

Las Vegas! That's where she went. Donna squinted to see the clock on the mantle without success. Then she glanced at her phone, remembering it constantly kept track of time. It was less than two hours. No way she'd be able to fly there. The price alone would be astronomical. It would take four hours to fly and that was a straight shot. There never seemed to be straight shots from Ashville. Why did her mother even invite her if they couldn't make it?

The phone in Donna's hand rang. It was Maria. "Did you get an invitation to the wedding, too?" Donna asked.

"I did," Maria confirmed.

"Why would they even bother to invite us when we can't get there? It's just cruel." Donna had missed her mother's first wedding due to the fact she hadn't been born or even thought about, for that matter. She didn't want to miss this one.

"Donna," Maria started with a slightly amused tone, "did you even bother to read the entire message? They are streaming the wedding in real time. It's an invitation to *watch.*"

Not an invitation to be at the wedding, but to watch the wedding, via a link in the text message? If Ten eavesdropped on their conversation, he'd refer to her as a Luddite again. At one point, he listened in history class. The Luddites were against technology. However, technology at that time was the weaving machinery in factories. Besides, she wasn't a Luddite. She appreciated all types of technology, even though she wasn't the best with many of them.

A quick head swivel revealed no one knew about her missing the wedding link unless she counted Maria. Usually only royal weddings were broadcasted, but she had heard of streaming wedding ceremonies. If she hadn't been so consumed by the murder, she would have noticed the link, which was even a different color, so it was clickable. Her lips pursed as she blew out a long breath.

"Link, huh. No, I was ready to see if there were any direct flights, which I'm sure there aren't. Even if they did, we couldn't have gotten there in time."

"I'm just thankful it's a link. I wouldn't want to take Baby Cici on a plane. You know how people can get about a crying baby."

Was her sister-in-law referring to her? More than once, she'd complained about the lunacy of bringing a baby on the plane. Maria always pointed out that often the mother had no choice. "Yeah. People can be jerks." Anxious to get off a subject where she'd just labeled herself a jerk, she asked, "What did you have in mind?"

"I thought we could all watch it on the big television at the inn. We could make a party of it. Wouldn't that be fun?" Maria's laughter, high and airy, resembled windchimes, the smaller, quality ones. "I don't even have to see you to know you're making that scrunched up face you make when someone suggests something, and you think you'll end up doing all the work"

"I didn't say that." She may have thought it, but knew good and well she didn't share the sentiment. "I guess it will be fun."

Maria sighed, then added, "Good. I already texted Daniel to meet us at the inn. My laptop and dress are already in the car."

"We have to dress for the wedding?" Donna had already changed out of her baking show outfit. Another clothes change and she might rival a duchess for the most clothes changes in a day, especially if she counted changing into her pajamas.

"I think it would be nice. We could take photos. Cecilia would like that."

Donna closed her eyes, wondering why everything always happened at once. "Yes, she would." It would make her mother feel more like they participated in the event. "How about food?" She waited a beat, hoping Maria would suggest something but everyone expected her to cook. Donna added in a resigned tone, "I guess I could dig through the freezer and see what I have."

"Don't. I thought we could order Chinese. Simon and Cecilia are having an unconventional wedding, we might as well spring for unconventional wedding food."

"It wouldn't be unconventional for a Chinese wedding."

"Now you're getting into the spirit. I'm going to drop by the bakery and pick up a small cake. Your part will be to chill the champagne and see if you can find anything in the storage shed that's wedding appropriate."

"No worries. I have plenty in the shed waiting for a lucky couple who want to celebrate their vows at the inn. I don't think we'll be using the bridal arch, though. Apparently, Heloise started this whole runaway wedding with her remark of seeing Cecilia leave Simon's home at an unusual hour." She punctuated the sentence with a derisive snort. "I have half a mind to call her and invite her to the wedding."

"Don't!"

Her sister-in-law still couldn't tell when Donna was serious or kidding. The last person she'd invite would be Heloise. If the woman couldn't pick at Cecilia for the time being, she'd start on someone else. Donna didn't have the energy to stomp out any rumors Heloise might start. "No worries. I was only joking, you know."

Maria's sigh of relief carried over the phone. "Well, I'm off. I contacted Daniel. You make sure to call Mark and Ten, so they can be there on time. Sloane, should we call her, too?"

"Yes. They are back on again. To not invite her would upset Ten." Donna anticipated Maria's next request. "I'll notify her, too. Not sure if she'll have to work. Mom is sure waiting to the last minute to let us know."

"It's cute. They're like teenagers in love who run off to get married in another state."

"If they were teenagers in love, they'd end up living with one or the other's parents. That's not happening. My mother wanted her wedding to be original, and I'm betting this one will be. I have no clue what they'll do. She might have showgirls as bridesmaids or Siegfried and Roy might officiate."

"We have less than two hours to find out. Do you think she meant her time or our time?"

Donna assumed she meant their time. "I thought it was our time, but I don't really know. I'll text her to be sure and will let you know. See you soon."

"Same here."

Donna stood motionless for a moment deciding what she should do first. She spoke aloud to herself. "I'll text mother, then I'll hit the shed." She suited her actions to her words as she hustled toward the barn while pecking out a text message. When Ten's tall shadow fell across her while she moved a half-dozen boxes labeled *wedding chapel*, she let out a yelp and jumped.

"Sorry," Ten apologized. "I thought you knew I was behind

you."

"I do now" She pressed a hand to her rapidly beating heart. "I must have been making too much noise, trying to find something appropriate for Cecilia and Simon's wedding."

Ten cleared his throat and gave her a puzzled look. "You do know they aren't getting married here, right?"

"Of course, I do. I'm not stupid. I got the text. Did you get the text?"

"Yep. I'm here to make sure you understand about how to view the link and all."

It was sweet he wanted to help. Still, it chafed that everyone assumed if it involved technology, she was helpless. "I know how it works. Besides, everyone is coming over here to watch it on the big screen television. We're having Chinese food and making a party of it. Maria thinks everyone should dress up as if they were actually there. There will be champagne toasts and cake. Make sure to invite Sloane if you think she might like to come."

"I will. What time?"

That, she didn't know for sure. "Make sure you're here by six pm. Not sure if that is Vegas time or Legacy time. If nothing else, we can eat Chinese food and play canasta until it's time."

Ten held his hand up. "I got a message." He pulled out his phone, glanced at it, and grinned. "It's six o'clock our time. Your mother texted me back. She wants to be sure you got the message."

"I *can* use a phone. Now she's just being cruel. For all I know, Simon typed the message in for her. I do know that doesn't leave me much time to find some wedding appropriate decorations. You can help me."

Donna pulled the flaps from one box and lifted out a large silk floral arrangement consisting of white lilies, pink rosebuds, baby's breath, and green leatherleaf. "Here, you can hold this."

In another box, she found a statuette of two white doves gazing at each other in adoration, then, some flat paper bells that unfolded to make a white bell that could be hung. Even though the bride and groom wouldn't be with them, she still picked out the glasses with *Bride and Groom* written in script on two glasses. "Okay, I think that will do it."

It took some major rushing around to get the second parlor ready for the wedding. Maria showed up with a cake and Baby Cici by five-thirty. Her brother trooped in five minutes later still attired in his construction clothes, dripping sawdust everywhere he walked. Maria solved the problem by handing him his clothes and directing him to the guest bathroom. Mark hadn't shown, nor had he responded to her message. It looked as if he might miss the wedding. What a shame. Her mother would be so disappointed. Donna rushed into the bedroom to change clothes. If need be, she'd lie and Photoshop Mark into the photos later, possibly with Ten's help.

She hit her bedroom at a jog. The floral chiffon dress, along with the hat she decided to wear, waited on the bed. With no time to spare, she kicked off her shoes and was in the process of pulling the top over her head when she recognized the creak of the bathroom door opening. Uncertainty froze her in place. There shouldn't be anyone in the bathroom. What if it was someone who decided to eliminate another contestant? Currently, as the front runner, she'd be the one more likely for someone to get rid of. Mark kept his pistol in the bedside table. All she had to do was get it without alerting her assailant.

Donna yanked down her top and lunged across the bed to reach the bedside table as fast as possible. An ominous crinkle and crunch meant her smart hat was no more. Her fingers grasped the metal pull on the drawer and yanked it open. Inside, there laid a current mystery her husband was reading, some cough drops, and some Chapstick. Where was the gun?

"What are you doing?" a very familiar voice demanded.

The breath she had been holding made its way through her tight lips as she turned and regarded her husband, whose hair was still damp from the shower. He buttoned up a clean shirt and angled his head to the drawer. "What did you hope to find in there that was so all important?"

"A gun."

He nodded as if that made perfect sense. "What happened to yours?"

She *did* have one, but she had locked it in the safe to keep it from falling into the wrong hands, mainly a guest's. "It's locked up."

"You need mine? Why?" He tucked his shirt into his pants, then buckled his belt.

"I thought you were a murderer coming to kill me." She released a long breath, then took another. Relieved certain death didn't loom on her agenda, she switched the subject. "I won the scone test today."

He raised his eyebrows as opposed to mentioning that she had reacted instead of using logic. "I wouldn't worry about anyone trying to kill you off because of your delicious scones. Also, congratulations on the win. Not sure if you heard me yelling way to go, Donna. Unfortunately, with most of the town watching the show, someone decided to break into the print shop and Debby's Downhome Cupcakes."

He shook his head as if he couldn't believe the perfidy of criminals who would take advantage of a distracted community. "It's my opinion that whoever killed Emily had a personal beef or was a hired assassin. I'm leaning toward the first. She must have known and trusted her killer to let him in. As for the killer, there're so many ways he could have killed her. The fact he chose to use his hands suggests a great deal of rage at Emily."

"I agree."

The was a rapid knock on the door. "It's starting," Ten called out.

Donna and Mark rushed out of the room with Mark snagging a tie from the closet as they did so.

The sound of Elvis singing *Love Me Tender* floated down the hallway. Ten followed them with his own commentary. "I'm not sure why I had to change when you didn't."

"I will change right before the photos. I ran out of time fixing up the parlor," she explained, as she followed the music into the second parlor where Maria perched with the baby on her knee. They were both attired in yellow dresses decorated with random colorful flowers. It must have been part of a Mommy and Me collection.

Daniel stood beside the television watching a tall Elvis in a black, rhinestone jumpsuit sing as he led their mother up the aisle. Cecilia was resplendent in a shimmery red cocktail dress with a lace jacket. Her mother looked great in anything she wore, but she had a feeling the color was a jab at Heloise. It wouldn't surprise her if her mother would have the photo of herself, Simon, *and* Elvis printed in the local paper.

Simon waited at the altar with the minister with an approving look directed toward his bride. Elvis, or the man pretending to be Elvis, handed Cecilia to Simon while pretending to be devastated that he had to. He then immediately broke into a song about a girl being his lucky charm.

The minister waited until the entertainer was done before reciting the service. The two seniors acted as thrilled as any twenty-year-olds would be, being serenaded by an Elvis impersonator. They were probably more excited because Elvis would have been their contemporary. Who knows? Her mother might have even attended some of his early concerts.

A tear found its way down her cheek as she watched the two exchange rings. To think her mother hadn't expected to ever find love after the death of Donna and Daniel's father. Mark reached for her hand, entwining his fingers with hers. Sloane left her position next to the wall to offer Donna a tissue from the box she was holding.

The minister pronounced them husband and wife, and the couple turned toward the camera with big grins. Simon announced, "We did it!"

Cecilia held up her left hand and declared, "I married the best man in the world!"

An unfamiliar voice announced, "Weddings always make me cry. Reminds me of when my husband and I got married."

Donna turned to see Marjorie Holmes, her guest *and* fellow competitor. Elvis broke into song again, this time about fools falling in love, which didn't seem entirely appropriate for a wedding.

"Me, too," Sloane announced and passed the tissue box.

Her mother's disappearance had turned into a happily-ever-after ending.

The doorbell rang. Guests wouldn't bother ringing the bell. It had to be dinner. "I'll get it. Decide if you want to eat in here or the dining room. Donna hurried to the door as she pondered what to do with Marjorie. Maybe the woman would drift on, realizing she had stumbled on to a private event. When Donna returned with two grocery bags full of food from The House of Good Fortune, Mark was handing Marjorie a champagne flute. He probably felt sorry for her, mistaking her for a lonely widow.

If nothing else, she might find out how Marjorie was chosen for the show and if she had met Emily before.

Chapter Fifteen

D ONNA ASSEMBLED WHITE stoneware plates and the better cloth napkins. It might be take-out, but it was still her mother's wedding feast. If they would be dining in the parlor, she needed to remind everyone to use a coaster. She certainly bought plenty for that purpose. A relieved sigh escaped her as she tucked the napkins into the pocket of an apron she had thrown on. They needed flatware, too. No plastic forks that broke whenever you stabbed anything. Maria would take photos of everything and no plastic implements would be in any of them.

The forks and spoons went into additional pockets, weighting her apron down. It made Donna feel a little bit like the servers she encountered in the inexpensive eateries who kept all the needed implements, including menus, on their person. Usually, the prospect worried the nurse in her due to the germs. At least she knew her apron was freshly laundered.

Donna balanced the plates in one cradled arm and used her right hand to open the door. When Ten spotted her, he hurried out into the hall and took the plates from her. The boy—she mentally corrected herself—the *man* was growing up. Things would work out with him and Sloane, she just knew it.

The long butler table she had put in front of the couch served as a buffet table. The distinctive black and white takeout containers crowded the surface. A quick glance reminded her. She had forgotten the serving spoons. Daniel, her brother, leaned against the wall doing absolutely nothing. "Brother, dear?"

"What do you want?" Even though the question might have been abrupt, it was softened by his amused tone.

"Serving spoons." She counted the items on the table. "I think eight. No. Make it ten."

"Ten, it is."

Her brother shuffled on his assignment as Marjorie made her way to Donna. The woman flashed her a genuine smile. "Your family told me your mother eloped to Las Vegas to get married. How exciting!"

"Yes, it was." No need to mention it was more than a little exciting. They couldn't figure out where her mother had gone at first.

Marjorie tapped her fingers on her chest. "My first husband and I slipped off to Vegas, too, for a quickie wedding."

The word *quickie* made it sound somehow less than a wedding a person had spent years planning and taking out a second mortgage to pay for. Even though Donna wanted to object to her mother's wedding being lumped in with other *quickie* weddings, she said nothing. After all, hadn't she read somewhere that the less spent on a wedding the better chance it had of being successful.

"I'm surprised they didn't put that in your bio."

Not understanding that Donna was serious, Marjorie nodded her head. "They should have. My Walter dressed up as Captain Kirk. Since I had the legs for it, I wore one of those mini dresses with go-go boots."

"You're a fan?"

"Good heavens, no! We were in Vegas, had a bit too much to drink, and we heard about the place. They have costumes you can change into. I heard the chapel is closed now, but they open it up whenever they have a Star Trek convention in town. Besides, it's a lot harder to get married in Vegas now. I tried it with my second husband, and you have to wait two weeks for the paperwork to go through."

"That must have been a pain for you." *Two weeks.* That meant her mother was planning to slip away the entire time she had counseled Ten. Her worker hadn't encouraged her to do something wild because her mother had already cooked something up.

"No, not at all. We headed to Mexico, which is much prettier than Vegas. Got hitched by some minister who mumbled the whole service in Spanish. Not sure if it was even legal. I guess it didn't matter. ZZ got kicked in the head by a mule and died. He looked like a member of the band ZZ Top, hence the name. He left me his chopper motorcycle."

The woman was certainly chatty, and her actual life bore no resemblance to a typical grandmother's. "You have had an interesting life. Did you marry your Captain Kirk before you were an Army nurse?"

Before she could answer, Mark topped off Marjorie's champagne flute. which she drank in one swallow and burped. "I was never an Army nurse. It sounded interesting, especially the part of me piloting the helicopter. When those guys showed up at the bakery and coffee shop where I worked and asked me if I wanted to be on television, I jumped on it. I had no clue they were going to make me into something I wasn't. Personally, I've had a pretty interesting life. I have a good voice, too."

In an effort to demonstrate, she broke into song, singing about being in love with a hard-hearted woman. "Still got the pipes. I even sang back-up in Nashville. Not traveling with a group, but in a studio. I sang with the Everly Brothers, Patsy Cline, and Bob Dylan, although I may have been cut from the last one. He liked to go it alone. Don't you think that would make for a more interesting bio than working with rescue dogs?"

Good question. Donna assumed Marjorie would want to know her actual life was more riveting than the saint-like profile they created for her, but her pondering the subject gave Marjorie more time to plead her case. She held out her flute for a refill as she spoke. "I know this is the South and they thought a traditional grandmother would work better down here. Still, I got my own women's Bible study group. We meet Saturday mornings at the bakery, guzzle some coffee, wolf down some donuts and pastries, then hit the road on our hogs."

An image of a group of church ladies straddling sizable porkers came to mind, although Donna was fairly certain it wasn't the case. "Bikes?"

"Motorcycles. Harleys. You remember me telling you about Wilbur?"

Actually, she hadn't. Donna was tempted to start counting Marjorie's husbands on her fingers to keep things straight. "I must have been out of the room."

The rest of the crowd helped themselves to food while Marjorie spun out her life story. She raised an eyebrow at Donna. "You were here. Remember ZZ? His long beard and his resemblance to the group."

"ZZ Top," Donna finished for her. "I was here for that."

"Anyhow, he left me his bike, a specialty one, too. I learned how to ride it. Once I got the hang of it, I wanted someone to ride with me. I founded my own all-women's bike club. On the back of our jackets is W.O.W. and a pig reading a Bible."

Donna knew she'd be sorry, but she had to ask, "What does

W.O.W. stand for?"

"Women of the Word, of course," Marjorie said with a smirk as if everyone would naturally know that and chugged her third glass of champagne.

Even though Donna hadn't had a chance to toast Simon and her mother's wedding or enjoy any fried wontons, she might have to forgo it to keep Marjorie talking. On the other hand, if she didn't eat anything, that would appear odd, too. Because she was hungry, she loaded up on fried rice, lo mein, sweet and sour pork, and beef broccoli. She managed to squeeze in an eggroll and some wontons on top. Instead of grabbing the provided chopsticks, she went with a fork. She actually wanted to finish before midnight. She enjoyed a few bites of eggroll, and there was a general discussion about the wedding, which should be expected, but it kept Marjorie from contributing, and she hadn't told Donna what she needed to know.

Donna perched on one of the extra folding chairs they had brought in for the wedding and waved her half-eaten egg roll as if it were a wand. "What made you leave your bakery job to be in the show?"

"I haven't left it. Just took some vacation time. Even if I stay for the entire six shows, it's only a week. Besides, I get five hundred dollars for every show, plus my stay at the inn is paid for. It's more than I get paid at the bakery. I even got in a walk at the beach today and nibbed around in some shops. So, it's a vacation in a way."

Even though Marjorie continued to ramble about the various things she did that day, all Donna could do was think about the money. Five hundred was nothing to sneeze at. It sounded as if she needed to ask the producer where her money was. Still, it wouldn't make sense to kill someone for five hundred. Most cell phones cost more than that or at least that's what the service provider tells customers when they lose or break one.

Time could work for her or against her. Donna enjoyed her food while Marjorie did likewise. Her sister-in-law passed off the baby to Daniel and pulled out her camera.

"Don't take any of me. I haven't had time to change."

"You know how to fix that," Maria announced and took a photo when Donna was shoveling food in her mouth.

Her first instinct was to jump out of her seat and grab the phone from Maria to delete the photo. To think she initially thought Maria shy and polite when she first met her. Her sister-in-law had changed over the years, or maybe Donna's perception had. Not wanting to play the part of a shrew, Donna settled for a grimace while she plotted to delete her own image from the phone when Maria wasn't paying attention.

Mark picked up one of the open champagne bottles and made a circuit around the room, filling up glasses. "What does a person win if they're crowned head baker?"

"That's the rip," Marjorie commented and wrinkled her nose. "While we all get paid for being on the show, there's no grand prize like a half million dollars or a car." She shook her head as if she could hardly believe it herself. "I know Bob hoped the place would be good advertising for his restaurant. The way the emcee and the judges run off at the mouth, Bob never even got to mention his restaurant."

"I know that feeling. Do the others have similar reasons?"

Marjorie stopped in mid-sip as she considered the matter. "Harley wants to be an actress, if you couldn't tell. I'd assume Dalton wants the free advertising, but he'll need to work hard to get the name of his place out. Prashant is a puzzle."

It sounded like whoever contacted the various contestants told them whatever they needed to hear to put on the show. Obviously, there was no contest, and there would be no winner. "Did you have any other reason you wanted to be on the show, besides a paid vacation?"

"A husband, of course. There are men out there, but not so many where I live, and I've been out with every single one of them. There's a reason they're single. No self-respecting woman would have them. I explained to the producers, or whatever they were, that I need to look good. Can't catch a husband looking my age. I guess they made *you* the frumpy housewife instead."

"Yes, they did." It explained why she had to wear the Mama wig.

Tipsy with too much champagne, Marjorie broke into giggles. "You showed them when you ripped off the wig and fluffed up your hair. Every person sitting in the audience probably thought the producer planned it that way."

A derisive snort came from Mark, drawing all eyes. He held up his hands as if in surrender. "Come on. Donna has lived in this town all her life. Those who know her, which everyone does, wouldn't be surprised by anything she does."

Really? This is what he thought of her? "Ten, get me something non-greasy I can throw at Mark. Make sure it isn't heavy. I don't want to break anything, either."

A pillow landed near her feet. Donna placed her half-eaten plate under her chair and picked up the pillow. "Now you're in trouble."

"Hey!" Mark crossed his hands in front of his face. "I was just pointing out how unique you are. If you were ordinary, like almost everyone else in this town, you wouldn't have been so interesting."

Donna had her arm up in a throwing position as she contemplated what he said. "*Unique* is usually what you say when someone gives you food you don't like. I'll let it go—this time"

A pillow came from another direction and bounced off Mark's face. Mark glared at Donna who shook the pillow still in her hand. Using his incredible deductive skills, he gazed over the assembled group, settling on the culprit. Marjorie giggled.

"I nailed him good for you, Donna!"

Ah, it sounded like the first gesture of friendship. Maybe she and Marjorie would become good friends. That way, the woman could spill the beans about all she knew. Personally, Donna had a feeling she'd already done that. However, sometimes people know stuff they don't realize they know. The hard part was getting the right information out of them.

Chapter Sixteen

T HE ELEGANT HOSTS and judges from "The Great British Bake Off" show were in the front row of Legacy's audience. Obviously, the producer placed them to be seen clearly when the camera panned the audience. It made her wonder who had been ousted from their seats. No matter. The challenge recipe was a fruit tart. Normally, it was an easy one if the crust was light enough. There was some cardboard and pie filling masquerading as a fruit tart in this very city. What she needed was something to distinguish herself from the cherry and apple fruit tarts she knew would be in the competition.

With a smile, Donna went right to work. A lemon meringue would wow the judges. A tiny, perfect lemon meringue. Most people avoided meringue in a humid climate like Legacy, but Donna had her secrets. Besides, it wasn't like the meringue would wait around very long. She would finish it right before her time was up. She whizzed through the crust using ice for extra flakiness. Next was the filling, which was another win. What she needed for the meringue were extra egg whites. This was day three of the competition and her egg count was depleting fast, but she had enough for today. With luck, maybe tomorrow would be just a biscuit, and not the British kind, either.

Victory was so close she could smell it, and it smelled like lemon meringue tart. A blast of cold air ruffled her hair as she peered into the fridge and saw nothing. No butter. No fruit. And worst of all, no eggs. "Where are my eggs?"

Seeing victory so close only to have it snatched away stung. A plain lemon tart would be okay, but not a show stopper. Donna stood stunned. A quick glance revealed the front row guests giving her pitying looks. She could even hear one of the British guests comment. "I'm not sure why we're even here. What do Yanks know about baking anyhow?"

This must have been how Bob felt when the flour exploded on him. Donna inhaled deeply. It was time to put on her big girl panties and see how she could salvage her lemon tarts. She peered in the cabinet where the dry goods were stored. The only thing in there was an almost empty bottle of cinnamon. Where had her supplies gone? A buzzing sound filled her head. Her hand went up to touch her brow and found it dry and cool. Weird. People often reported hearing buzzing before they fainted.

Something landed on her shoulder and shook it. "Donna, it's your phone. Answer it. This is the second time. Whoever is trying to reach you won't give up."

"Huh?" What was Mark doing in the test kitchen?"

"Your phone."

Donna patted below her waist for a phone and discovered she had no pockets. The material felt silky. Good heavens. What was she wearing? Panic settled in her throat, making it hard to breathe and also reminded her of the dreams she had where she'd gone to school in her pajamas. Her eyelids flickered open to grayness, illuminated by the tiny red lights of a few electrical items charging. The image disoriented her at first. It was so different from the bright, sunny, test kitchen. Once she realized she was in her own bedroom and there wasn't an egg crisis, she let out a long, relieved breath.

The phone that had stopped ringing began again.

"Donna," Mark reminded her.

"I'm getting it. Not sure who needs to call this early." She found her phone by feeling the bedside stand, then swiped to the right to answer. "Hello?"

"Is this Donna Tollhouse Tabber?"

"Taber," she corrected.

"You're late for your makeup call. How can you expect to look frumpy if you aren't here on time?"

"I don't want to look frumpy." That should have been obvious from the previous show. "We're still filming? I heard Agatha went to the emergency room." Donna stopped short of saying poisoning. It might not be a well-known fact.

"We have a replacement judge. Get here fast." A click and the sound of nothingness followed, which meant the call had ended for all intents and purposes.

Show biz folks had no manners. Donna's feet met the rug beside the bed as she played with the idea of doing her hair. She was late already, they might not do her hair or worse, stick one of those itchy wigs on her head. Who knows who wore it last? For all she knew, mice could have set up residence in the wig box.

It took less than ten minutes to get dressed even with the few minutes she sacrificed to the flat iron. Legacy wasn't some sprawling metropolis with bumper to bumper traffic. She was only, technically, twenty minutes late. No one appreciated how fast she managed to jump out of bed and make it to the commons where the filming took place. Mona griped the entire time she did her makeup, which was a scant five minutes.

Donna blinked at her image in the mirror. "I'm a natural blonde. I need some color. Feel free to cut loose with the eye shadow or blush."

The mirror reflected Mona with her arms crossed and lips pressed into a line. Donna had assumed from their first meeting that the makeup artist tended to be overwhelmed easily. The woman in the mirror with her muscular arms and surly attitude would make a decent bouncer. Mona shook her head no, then added, "You ruined all the work I did yesterday. I'm not wasting my time on you today."

A petulant makeup artist wasn't good business. Still, Donna knew enough about people to know no more makeup would be forthcoming. At least she had brought her own, which was back in the trailer. It was a quick countdown to broadcast. Donna rushed back to the trailer and left the door standing open to hear any calls for the contestants to be on the set as she enhanced her face.

The loudspeaker blasted the emcee's smarmy patter into the trailer, causing Donna to wrinkle her nose in reaction. Did people even believe him? He was as fake as Leona Buell's dentures. The difference was Leona didn't care if people knew her teeth were fake. In fact, she sometimes pulled them out of her mouth if anyone wanted a closer look. The memory of her mother's friend handing her a set of teeth made her grin as she added another coat of mascara. The emcee explained another change.

"Our own lovely Agatha had to step down for medical reasons." There was a prolonged *Oh!* from the audience, which was replaced by low murmuring.

Yeah, sometimes people did call poisoning a medical issue. Donna went on to add blush and a brighter lipstick. Most teenagers could have done a better job on the makeup than Mona did. For all her talk about wanting to work in Hollywood, the girl didn't have the skills. Donna had seen the grocery tabloids that featured stars without their makeup and decided Hollywood makeup artists had to be the closest thing to miracle workers she'd ever witnessed. Obviously, no one on the show was authentic, excepting herself, of course.

The emcee continued with forced enthusiasm. "We are proud to announce one of your own has stepped forward to be a judge, a local restaurateur."

Well, that left a good sixty or so possibilities. As a vacation destination, Legacy had plenty of cafés that offered sandwiches, ice cream, specialty coffees, and sodas. Calling them restaurants would be about the same as calling a unicycle a bike. They were both missing vital parts.

"You may recognize your new judge because of her restaurant's appearance on the Food Network."

That narrowed down the possibilities. She couldn't think of anyone who had been on the Food Network, except for Janice's restaurant, The Croaking Frog. Donna pursed her lips as she heard her friend's voice thanking everyone for coming today. If Janice was the judge, they might as well cut to the chase and give her the trophy or silver-plated cake stand or whatever the winner received right now. Her friend wouldn't be drawn into some scam to crown a pre-selected winner. If nothing else, Janice was all about taste.

Her life just got easier. With Janice as a judge, she could concentrate on finding out more about Emily and about Agatha's ingestion of arsenic. Even though Agatha was fairly pale, she doubted the woman was swallowing arsenic to keep her skin lily white as they did in the 1700s. That meant someone had it out for Agatha, but not necessarily the same person who killed Emily. A previous case taught her not to contribute all deaths or near deaths to the same person.

Poison used to be called a woman's weapon. It was generally

assumed that women, as the weaker sex, could never knife or shoot another person. Hand to hand combat was out. The gentler sex could poison and be on their way before death actually occurred, sparing them from witnessing the end result of their actions.

A fast-moving crew member knocked on her trailer wall since the door was open. "Contestants to the test kitchen!"

This was it. Even though her initial goal had been not to look frumpy, the oversized apron had benefits. They came in the form of two huge pockets that were big enough to hide the extra eggs she brought. A lingering remnant of her dream had her sneaking in eggs and an extra container of cinnamon that she palmed in her hand. Let's hope she wouldn't have to shake hands before she made it to her station.

Marjorie gave Donna a friendly wave. They bonded over Cecilia and Simon's Vegas wedding. In an effort to not break the eggs, Donna chose not to use her normal ground eating stride. Instead, she chose her steps carefully, hoping to appear graceful as opposed to being on her way to the senior center. Janice, instead of acknowledging her, gave her a blank stare. At least the bread guy managed a cheerful expression. Each contestant drifted to their station. Harley wore a denim skirt, gingham blouse, and cowboy boots. She had a black scarf dotted with something white wrapped around her head like a headband with the two ends sticking up like a bow or tiny bunny ears.

The skirt was about six inches too short in Donna's opinion. It could be that Harley's character changed into a sexy country girl. The producer must be tweaking the show to keep people interested. She knew Marjorie's story and most of Bob's, but she knew nothing of Harley's. So far, the girl showed no skills in the kitchen. If Harley wasn't cute, young, and curvy, Donna might wonder why she was picked.

Prashant took his place without saying a word. Still, his very presence drew Donna's attention. If he had tried to kill Agatha, why was he still around? Maybe because a sudden departure sometimes was almost as good as a confession. Most people believed that innocent people wouldn't hit the road. Some did. Smart criminals stayed and pretended it was just another day.

The area around the outspoken baker's eyes was caked with makeup. It was an obvious attempt to hide something. Those in the studio audience probably wouldn't notice, but it was hard to miss closeup. Did he have a black eye or two? Did Agatha scratch him? So far, Prashant was the more likely candidate to have poisoned Agatha. There was no motive to poison Emily, however.

She always assumed everyone had a believable motive.

Her love of television crime dramas taught her that sometimes there were crazy people in the world who kill others for no discernable reason. Donna cut her eyes to Prashant, who was fussing with his shirt. He must have felt her gaze and met her stare with a steady one of his own. No madness in the eyes, although he did look tired, maybe even puffy around the eyelids.

He could have gotten some of the arsenic in his system. Red or swollen skin was a sign of poisoning. That might explain the makeup and the puffiness. Part of her wanted to warn him to seek medical treatment right away. Then again, he could be a stomach sleeper, which would explain the puffy eyes.

The emcee employed his extra syrupy voice and asked Janice, "What's on the menu today?"

"Cheesy biscuits." Janice spoke directly to the camera. "My restaurant is famous for its cheesy biscuits that come free with every meal. I even have people who want to buy some to take home with them. They are that good. It's no wonder The Croaking Frog was featured on the Food Network."

Mercy! She couldn't believe it. Not the cheesy biscuits. They were indeed good. No, it was the fact Janice got to plug her own business without being cut off. Maybe she was paying the show instead of getting paid.

The rattle of pans meant the other contestants were already assembling the needed supplies before the instructions were even announced. If she didn't get busy, she would be the one eliminated.

"All right, bakers!" the emcee announced, possibly unaware that almost every cook had turned on their ovens and were already measuring out the flour. "Your goal is to create a baker's dozen of cheesy garlic biscuits. You have thirty-five minutes. Go!" He waved his arm as if he were at the auto races.

Thirty-five minutes was cutting it close. It took about ten minutes of prep and another fifteen baking, assuming all your ingredients were measured and your oven was at the proper temperature. This was a sprint as opposed to a marathon.

Donna checked her oven to make sure it was heating properly. The next step was the batter. Normally, she liked to measure and assemble the ingredients to make sure she hadn't forgotten anything vital. She adopted this technique when one morning she forgot the orange juice for the orange chicken. It turned out okay, but mediocrity was not what she was aiming for. She'd measure as she went. There were less than eight ingredients.

She cradled the mixing bowl as she reviewed the recipe in her head. Her version was only for nine, and they weren't very big biscuits. The Croaking Frog didn't serve big biscuits. The bread was already free. The assumption was people would order a full meal, the price making up for the biscuits. No way would she begrudge the woman a smaller than normal biscuit. Every business person had to protect their bottom line.

Once the dry ingredients were assembled, she added the milk and only stirred enough to moisten the biscuit dough. Over stirring made it less airy and sometimes flat. Donna had her biscuits in the oven with time to spare. That allowed her to contemplate which contestant might be the murderer. Bob was already out, which would have given him no reason to poison. Marjorie, while interesting, didn't strike her as a killer. All the woman wanted was another husband. She knew there was no prize at the end and had no hopes of becoming an actress or a model.

Harley was young, possibly strong, but didn't strike Donna has being overly clever. However, she could be an excellent actress pretending to be limited. As for Prashant, it was hard to say. Without knowing why someone killed Emily, it was hard to pin it on anyone. Most people would think the ex-husband was guilty. Why would he kill his ex-wife? They'd already divided up the goodies. She doubted that Emily left whatever she owned to her ex, even though from what little she read in Emily's journal, she still loved him. It could be possible she left everything to Dalton. Maybe Mark could find out something about Emily's will. Where were her relatives? Who was picking up the body? Dalton identified the body but implied Emily's parents would be coming. She needed to check on that with Mark.

While the other contestants dashed around, Donna remained confident in her recipe. It was the one she gave Janice for her restaurant's memorable biscuits. Prashant was a wild card she needed to know more about. His station would take six large steps to reach. Not close enough to hear anything, but what would she expect to hear? The man murmuring his guilty secrets for the world to hear? Even so, she sidestepped in his direction as far as she could in her cubicle.

No one would leave their station for fear of their biscuits burning. The actual baking was a major component on the British show. It didn't take a genius to know people preferred the baked goods not to be doughy or burnt. Apparently, there was an art to getting a cookie the exact same color on both sides. Of course, Donna would refer to such a cookie as *not* done. The secret was having the bottom only lightly browned.

It was odd the cast of the British show was here. It implied that they were on board with the cheap rip-off version of their show. But it could be just the opposite. Maybe they were here checking out the competition. Still, it would have been costly to fly everyone over here, when normally they would have sent only one person. Maybe it was some bizarre cross-promotion. After all, they were in the front row.

Her timer chimed as she debated how to start a conversation with Prashant. It would be interesting to learn the story behind his puffy face. It would also help to know how dear old Agatha was. She stooped to open her oven, releasing the heated aroma of cheesy garlic biscuits done to golden perfection. Donna carried the cookie sheet with her hot-pad mitten covered hands to the counter to cool.

The various buzzers went off around her making it sound more like a casino than a test kitchen. It also proved that the other contestants had no issue with the basic recipe. Maybe tomorrow would yield a true challenge. A cake would be nice. Possibly a multi-layer one with fruit filling. Her harvest cake would fit the bill, but it was usually a fall dessert. Who knows? Maybe they'd have a fall show, and she'd be invited back. As for now, she needed to work on the presentation.

She found a rustic basket in the cabinet and lined it with a gingham napkin she also located. Instead of going straight under the biscuit with the metal spatula, it was best to let the sheet come up to room temperature. It wouldn't take that long. If she rushed it, she could damage the bottom of the biscuit. Judges could be picky about that stuff. Her lips pursed as she considered Janice as a judge. Her friend could be picky, especially when it came to food. Most of Donna's family members might not believe it, but Janice could be more demanding than even herself. Her friend ran a restaurant every day while Donna only handled a few guests for breakfast. Those guests got what they got and didn't have the opportunity to choose from a menu.

The emcee cleared his throat but must have been unaware that the microphone was switched on. The gurgles and growls were broadcasted to the audience, resulting in titters and a few outright laughs. His face flushed the slightest, but he pushed ahead.

"Time's up, bakers!" He made a show of looking around at the contestants, but this time everyone had finished on time. "Put down that spatula or hot pad."

This was it. Once Janice picked her biscuits as being the best, it would establish her as the front runner. A runner came by and grabbed her biscuit basket and placed them on the table for the judges to sample. It was no secret to the audience who baked what. This time Harley had finished the recipe. As her basket went by, the edges of a skeleton scarf fluttered, and the scent of burned bread trailed behind.

Odd that the contest would have a skeleton napkin, which would be more appropriate for Halloween. A suspicion took form. Her competitor was missing her black and white headscarf. Donna put up her hand as if she were in school, ready to warn the judges they were about to partake of headscarf biscuits. No one called on her for the timely revelation. Instead, everyone was focused on the judges who approached the table loaded with the biscuit baskets.

Janice got to go first. She waved to the audience, which resulted in sudden applause for the local. She picked up a biscuit, bit into it, and held the morsel in her mouth. Donna could read her friend's body language well enough to know she wanted to spit it out. Instead, she said, "This biscuit is overcooked, salty, and somehow lacks the basic ingredients, cheese and garlic. I wanted to like it, but I couldn't."

Donna sucked in her lips, almost sure it was Dalton's. She would have thought a cheesy biscuit would suit his restaurant, but maybe having his ex-wife murdered put him off his baking game.

The bread judge gave Janice a surprised look. Maybe she'd stolen his line or they forgot to discuss who would play bad judge this time. The die was set, and Janice had something critical to say about each biscuit. If this was how she talked to her staff, it explained why she had such a hard time keeping employees.

When they finally made it to Donna's biscuits, even she was doubtful that Janice wouldn't find something wrong with them. By this time, they would be cold. Her cameraman motioned her forward, so he could do a close-up on Donna as the judges made their pronouncements. The bread judge took a bite and closed his eyes, then he opened them and finished off the biscuit.

"This is what I would expect from a place like The Croaking Frog. I would always have to have more. I might even forget to order the entrée." He laughed as if he'd amused himself.

Janice didn't laugh but picked up a biscuit instead. Fortunately, she didn't make a pained face. "This will do. I'd be willing to hire this baker for *my* restaurant."

This will do? Really? Personally, after Janice's snotty display, she was fairly sure she didn't want to work at The Croaking Frog. Maybe the producer told her to act all high in the instep. Donna schooled her face into a serene expression, ready to break into a gracious smile when her name was announced.

Donna edged her way toward the front, ready for them to call her name as the winner. The eggs she had put in her pocket weighed heavy, reminding her of their presence. She'd have to keep the apron on and not reveal their rounded shape. No way could she reverse back to her kitchen and put them in the fridge with the camera on her.

"Okay!" The emcee announced, "We have a winner."

Not wanting to look too confident, Donna waited for her name to be announced. Others weren't so patient as a swell of murmuring broke out from the contestants. One pushed past Donna, knocking her against the counter.

"It's me! I know it's me." Harley shouted the words as she ran to the front of the test kitchen where the judges stood.

"Um," Janice cleared her throat and pointed to the basket on the end. "Are these your biscuits?"

"No. Those are boring! I went for interesting as opposed to ordinary." She pointed to her basket, which happened to be the first one Janice tasted.

"In that case," Janice gave a small nod, "you didn't win."

The emcee saw this as a good time to butt in with a comment. "The tension thickens. Who is the cheesy biscuit winner?"

The bread judge held up Donna's basket. "Will the baker who made this basket please step forward."

This was it. Donna gave a final pat to her hair, pushed her shoulders back and strode confidently to the front. As she did so, something cold and slippery slid down her leg. *This couldn't be happening*. It didn't take Sherlock Holmes to realize an egg had busted when Harley pushed her aside. Maybe her apron would hide the problem.

Attitude was everything. Even though the egg had penetrated her clothes and was now stiffening on her skin, she moved forward with a wide smile, ready to shake Janice's hand. As she circled around the protective counters, her waist and below was out in full view of the public.

Bread guy rhapsodized a little more about her biscuits. Janice smiled at her, then her eyes dropped to the wet spot that was spreading on the front of her apron. A disgruntled Harley reappeared clutching a tiny bit of an eggshell. She aimed the hand with the eggshell in Donna's direction. "She cheated! She brought in ingredients."

"We didn't even use eggs!" They hadn't. How could it be cheating if she brought in something they hadn't used.

"Cheater!" Harley screamed the words.

The woman, besides not being able to cook, was a sore loser. Donna's intentions were to keep her cool and ride it out. Somehow being called a cheater brought out the inner child in her and the need to retaliate. "At least I didn't wrap my biscuits in a grimy scarf I'd worn on my head, like you did."

Janice made a gagging noise, covered her mouth, and ran off stage. While bread guy stared into the camera, he blinked a couple of times, then spoke. "Due to unusual circumstances, the biscuit winner is…" he paused and swiveled his head to regard the remaining contestants, "Prashant."

Chapter Seventeen

AN EXCITED PRASHANT jogged to the front of the kitchen where both the judge and emcee stood. Clipboard Girl nudged Donna while hissing in her ear. "You need to get off camera, now!"

She almost asked *why*. It was obvious the judge had panicked and called out the first name he could think of. Harley was out due to horrible biscuits and bad hygienic practices. Even though Donna felt it was unfair, she too was kicked to the curb. Prashant had even pointed out there was no mention of not bringing extras. She trotted along beside her handler, which is the way she thought of the girl. Once they got off camera, the officious female sighed heavily.

"I know conflict sells, but it's wearing me out."

Obviously, the woman was confusing her with Harley. "I'm not the drama queen. I'm the one who made prize-winning biscuits."

The woman chuckled, then pointed to Prashant, who grinned wide as he waved to the audience. Music came on, which signaled the show was at its end. Those at home would see credits while most of Legacy's citizens were heading home, a few determined to try their hand at cheesy-garlic biscuits. Prashant stayed front and center and waved as the people left. A few had enough manners to wave back as they went on their way.

The crew swarmed the test kitchen and disassembled what needed to be and put away what couldn't be left overnight. Crew members didn't say anything to the happy winner. They just moved around him, the same way they moved around any object in their way.

The folks from the front row were up and waving, which shifted Clipboard Girl into action. She stopped for a moment and spoke over her shoulder to Donna. "Come back tomorrow. Any other person would have been canned, but since you bring the laughs, you get to come back."

Who shouldn't come back? If life was fair, it would be that un-couth Harley who couldn't boil an egg. It probably wouldn't be, though. Prashant won the challenge, it couldn't be him. The man must have got a clue that his moment of glory was over since he stopped waving. William Shakespeare coined the idea that everyone had fifteen minutes of fame. Prashant's fifteen minutes was cut short by the closing credits.

An incredible idea popped into Donna's head. A smile still tugged Prashant's lips up as he made his way to the parking lot. Her window of opportunity might slam shut before she even had a chance to wiggle through it.

"Prashant! Wait up." She jogged after the biscuit winner. The remaining egg bounced in her pocket. She slipped her fingers inside the pocket and around the egg, pulled it out, and deposited it in the trash as she ran. What a waste, especially considering she only bought the free-range eggs after a few of her guests expressed alarm that she hadn't. They actually tasted better but did cost more, much more than regular eggs.

The young man had the courtesy to stop. A stitch in her side had Donna shoving fingers into her side to keep going. After running a mile, or what felt like it, she reached Prashant. "Oh, thanks for waiting. I want to take you to lunch. You deserve to celebrate your spectacular win."

"Thanks." He placed a hand on his chest, and his eyes glowed as he spoke. "It was pretty sweet. I figured I would be the one to go home today."

"Obviously not." She flung out a hand toward the town. "We could walk. There are several nice cafes. First, I need to stop by my car and get some wipes to clean up this egg mess."

"Okay," he agreed. "How did you get an egg in your pocket?"

Yeah, people would want to know. She needed an answer that would make her sound less like a cheater. "I run a bed and breakfast. Normally, I fix people breakfast. The early makeup call had me scooting out the place before anyone was up. I was rushing around trying to set up everything for breakfast. My assistant was going to fix breakfast for the guests." What a lie! "My hands were full, and I needed one extra egg, so I slipped it into my pocket and must have forgotten about it."

Mark would have sliced up her excuse in a heartbeat. It was too detailed. Too much info was always the sign of someone who needed a specific alibi to cover certain matters. Sometimes, they made sure to tell exact times to make sure everyone knew they couldn't have committed the murder. Who looks at their watch or phone before doing a task? At ten-fifteen, I was just getting into my bubble bath. When I got out, I heard the eleven o'clock news come on. Mark would have asked what the lead story was or what channel it was on. Not all stations broadcasted at eleven. No one would believe her flimsy egg in the pocket excuse.

Her companion pondered the possibility, then nodded. "That makes sense."

It didn't, but he could be gracious and pretend he believed her, since he won today's challenge. Donna forced a chuckle. "Embarrassing is what it is. Let's go get the wipes. Not sure why I bother.

Everyone in town already knows about my egg fiasco."

Prashant said nothing, possibly feeling there was no correct response to such a statement. Once she dabbed off the egg residue, picked the shells out of her pocket, and grabbed her wallet, she was ready to go. As they walked to the Garden Delight—a lovely bistro that featured alfresco dining in the middle of an herb garden— Donna did a running commentary on Legacy. She included everything from the beginning with the textile mills and even the Columbus Day festival, which had been renamed Historical Seafarer's Day due to the lack of actual documentation that Columbus had ever landed there.

If she learned anything from her husband about questioning skills, it was to bury the important question. She even imitated some of the various tourists and their pirate speech, which had Prashant laughing.

"I'm so happy you're laughing. You looked so sad this morning."

That cut him off in mid-laugh. He swallowed. Donna figured the method Mark had used with much success didn't work, at least not for her.

Prashant took a deep breath and spoke in such a soft voice that he was hard to hear. "I feel horrible about Agatha. She told me she was pulling out of the show."

Weird. "Why would she tell you? The two of you bickered on the show. I would think you would be the last person she'd call."

He stopped walking and allowed his mouth to open a tiny bit. "You believe that Agatha and I didn't get along?"

Donna gave a hesitant nod, not willing to point out the nasty remarks they both had made.

Her confirmation caused Prashant to beam and press his hands together. "I told Agatha I was no actor, but she encouraged me to try. All I had to be was testy, difficult, and let everything set me off."

"You did a great job."

"Good." He rocked up to his toes, then back down again. "The day keeps getting better and better. I only wish Agatha had been here to see me win."

Killers often left the scene. A few even faked their own deaths to throw off suspicion. Her nurse colleague had mentioned the arsenic level was far from lethal. "That's a shame. How do you and Agatha know each other?"

"She was my teacher at the culinary institute."

That meant both she and Prashant could cook, which might make them the only real chefs in the entire show. Donna didn't include herself in that analysis. *She* knew she could cook. Still, the show wasn't about chefs, but more about ordinary people who liked to putter around the kitchen.

"Oh, I guess she told you about the show?"

"She recommended me for the show."

This show was crooked nine ways to Sunday. "That's interesting." She gestured to an arch covered with ivy. "We're here."

The murmur of voices and the sound of flatware on china carried on the warm air. During late spring, which they were now in, the sign usually disappeared underneath the vegetation. The locals liked to think of the place as their little secret. It was good. Donna sometimes thought herself the queen of breakfast, but the husband and wife team who ran the café were lunch royalty.

A young woman with a ready smile, clean-scrubbed face, and wrapped in a floral butcher apron greeted them. "Welcome to Garden Delight. Table for two?"

"Yes," Donna answered before Prashant could. "Something close to the greenhouse would be nice."

A large, aging greenhouse squatted near the back of the garden and was closed in on one side by the actual restaurant. It was possibly the least desirable table, but it *was* private.

"Of course," the girl replied with a tiny spark of knowing in her eyes.

They followed her as Donna speculated on how soon it would be before Mark heard about her dining with a young stranger. Nothing worked better than the gossip mill in a small town. Her husband, knowing him, would have no doubts she was conducting some casual investigation on her own.

A small, white iron wrought table waited under a shade tree. Whimsical cushions showing smiling flowers and birds with ribbons padded the matching iron wrought chairs. Donna took her seat before Prashant tried to do the polite thing and help her with her chair. Mark did it to be polite. Someone Prashant's age would assume she needed the assistance.

With them both seated, the girl handed them menus. "Rachelle will be your server. Today's specials include a cantaloupe bisque, ginger carrot soup, salad sandwich on ciabatta bread, and mushroom asparagus quiche."

Donna opened her menu and used it as a shield to watch the departing hostess. She had her cell phone in her hand before she had even walked five feet away. Ah, small-town life. Either you loved it or hated it. Most of the time, she loved it. Right now, her job was to put Prashant at ease as she prospected for vital information.

"The ginger carrot soup is good. As is the cantaloupe bisque, but I doubt the melons are local."

"Salad sandwich?" Her companion inquired with a lifted eyebrow.

"It's a salad between two pieces of bread. They do it up right, though. They start with some mixed greens, layer paper thin tomatoes and cucumbers on top. They finish with a lovely dill sauce and carrot shreds. They will add goat cheese or avocado slices if requested."

"Sounds good." He gave a nod, then smiled. "It was very considerate of you to bring me to a vegetarian restaurant."

Vegetarian restaurant? She never thought of the place in that way. It was more of the fresh soup and great salad place in her mind, somewhere she went for a light lunch. Her eyes roamed the menu, looking for a mention of a juicy burger or chicken fried steak. *Nothing.* The only burger was a black bean one. How clever of the owner opening a vegetarian restaurant and forgetting to mention it.

"Are you a vegetarian?"

The question made him cough a little, and he shrugged his shoulders. "In theory, at least. I occasionally enjoy a rack of ribs." He blinked, or it may have been a wink, as he continued. "It has to be an out of the way place. I've sometimes used Uber Eats to have them brought to my apartment, so I'm not seen going into a rib place."

"Would it be such a big deal? Here in Legacy, it would be odd *not* to eat ribs."

He heaved a sigh. "It would. I'm a sous chef in a vegetarian restaurant in New York. It's a job, a good one. Many were vying for it. The right word in the right ear got me an interview. There would be more than one who would discredit me if they could. The head chef wouldn't care, but some of the customers would boycott the place if they thought their food was prepared by a carnivore."

"You're an herbivore with a slight yen for ribs." She wrinkled her nose, imagining customers protesting a rib-eating sous chef. More importantly, a pattern was forming here. "Let me guess who whispered the right words. Agatha?"

"You'd be right." Prashant nodded and gestured with his menu. "She worked hard to make sure her top students ended up somewhere appropriate. Their success reflected back on her and the school."

So far, everything sounded believable. Rachelle showed up with lime water, a specialty of the place. They never asked if people wanted their lime infused water. Instead, they just brought it. So far, she hadn't heard of any customers having a lime meltdown or a lime allergy. Locals who knew did occasionally request plain water or more often, sweet tea.

Donna went with the quiche and carrot soup while her companion decided to try the salad sandwich. He might be sampling for his own restaurant. It made sense. Donna often did the same whenever she ate out. So far, Agatha sounded like the kind of friend any up and coming culinary graduate would want. "Was the culinary institute in England?"

His brows knitted together as he answered, "Sanborn, New York. Why would you think it was in England?"

The accent had to have come from somewhere. What about all those comments about dear old England? What was up with that back and forth about the British colonists and all? Before she could ask, Prashant covered his lips and made a small moan. "I let the cat out of the bag. Agatha will be so upset when I tell her."

Yes, he did let the cat out of the bag and in more ways than one. Did no one actually earn their way into this show with their superior cooking skills? While Prashant could cook, he wasn't a baker. It appeared Agatha, with the fake accent, brought him along with her. What was the point? Those two were very chummy. Donna had been at the top of her class in nursing school, but none of her teachers made an effort to get her a job. They certainly didn't keep contact after school, either. She took a long sip of her lime water as she pondered possibilities.

Donna placed her glass on the table with a dull thud. She went in bold and quit dancing around the obvious. "Did you know Emily before the show?"

"No." Prashant looked down instead of meeting her eyes, and played with his water glass, turning it in circles as he spoke. "I never met her. I just heard she had left the show because of family issues."

He didn't mention she died, which meant he didn't know or was very, very clever. "Why did you agree to be on the show? Were you hoping to make a name for yourself? Start your own restaurant?"

A low chuckle sounded as he shook his head no. When he raised his gaze to meet Donna's, the happy winner expression was gone to be replaced by one of weary resignation. "Certainly not. If you would have asked me while I was in school, my answer would have been different. I had dreams of creating beautiful, mouthwatering dishes that both customers and critics would rave about."

She'd had similar dreams, too, but only about her bed and breakfast. "What happened?"

"Reality. Work. I had no clue what it was like to work in a profitable restaurant. It's a production line conducted in ninety-degree heat with all the sounds and the yelling. No matter how much you prep or how precise you are, there's always a customer sending something back."

"I know the feeling."

Prashant shot her a confused look.

"My inn. I make a lovely gourmet breakfast for the guests. Then we have a mixer on the weekends with small-plate items." Even though it was considerable work for her, it didn't compare to working in a restaurant kitchen. "Every now and then, I have someone complain about my not serving something. People must think I'm a mind reader. Maria specifically put on the reservation form that any food allergies or special diet requests had to be mentioned ten days in advance. That way I can plan my menu and get my shopping done." Donna sighed dramatically, which she decided was a bit too much. "Do they listen?"

A different employee wove through the empty tables, balancing a round, laden tray, and headed their way. Their food arrived just when Prashant had loosened up enough to talk about what was really happening.

Donna thanked the server and dug into it. The ginger gave the carrot soup just the right amount of zing to make it interesting. While the quiche was light and filling, it had a top note due to a spice she couldn't name. It wasn't nutmeg, but it had an earthy, slightly sweet taste. As she ran through her favorite spices to use with egg dishes, Prashant spoke.

"I came for a vacation. I had the days coming. Agatha assured me Legacy was a beautiful, coastal town. Told me with my expertise in the kitchen, the actual show would be a breeze. Then, we could enjoy the beach and do a little antiquing."

Why hadn't she seen it earlier? "You antique?"

"Not really. It's more of Agatha's thing." He shrugged. "I expected I'd be eliminated early on. Now I miss this elimination round. There's no way either you or Harley would be cut due to all the drama you both bring. Marjorie is the producer's pick to win."

How did he know that? She opened her mouth to ask, but before she could, Prashant kept talking.

"Agatha told me. She explained it could be like "American Idol" in that the singers who didn't win often did better than those who did. I mean, who didn't guess that after Marjorie's flattering bio."

"Yeah," Donna agreed with a chuckle. Only she wasn't thinking about Marjorie, instead her mind picked up on the fact that the only contestant not mentioned was Dalton. He'd be next on the chopping block. It made sense. He didn't bring much more to the show than a handsome face. She wasn't even sure if his biscuits were that good.

Chapter Eighteen

IT WAS ALREADY one o'clock when Donna waved goodbye to Prashant and climbed into her car to drive home. Her impromptu skullduggery had put her behind at the inn. It was bad enough she farmed out her guests to a nearby diner for breakfast. The least she could do was get their rooms cleaned in a prompt fashion. With any luck, Ten would have started on them. All he had left were final exams, and he had already taken a majority of them and passed. Universities wanted to make sure a graduate actually finished before they walked across the stage and accepted the very expensive diploma.

Due to Legacy's tourist influx, a police car waited at all the places Donna would have normally goosed the gas pedal a little. Goodness! Being on a show and running a business proved challenging. The whole reason she quit her nursing job was to concentrate on the inn. Maybe she should fix up some grab-and-go snacks since the guests missed her gourmet breakfast. One of the celebrating couples would leave this morning. She could make sure they had a chance to sample some of her cooking.

They had come to the mixer, but it wouldn't be enough to counter a review that mentioned no breakfast was served at The Painted Lady Inn. Even worse, time slipped away as she followed a Legacy police car driving the sedate speed limit. Her husband probably told all the officers in town about Donna's tendency to speed. The officer may have recognized her and pulled in front of her to slow her down. She wrinkled her nose. Now she was just being paranoid.

There were young adults crowding the sidewalk. Some wore shorts and t-shirts. A few of the girls were strolling in swimsuits, very tiny ones, and flip flops. They had to be Yankees. A true southerner would wait until June or the very last weekend in May to don a swimsuit. The light turned red, which forced her to stop as the gaggle of teenagers crossed. While many talked as they crossed, the last girl kept her eyes glued to her phone. She moved slowly, allowing the light to turn to green.

The profile reminded her of Sloane, Ten's sweetie. Why would she be hanging out with the tourists? It couldn't be Sloane. Surely her mother would have found such a flimsy excuse for swimwear and burned it. Donna did have the courtesy not to honk, but that wasn't the case for the car behind her. The girl looked up revealing it *was* Sloane—or her secret twin. A tear streamed down her face as she stared back at the cars.

Donna watched her hurry across the street to catch up with the rest of the group. This didn't look good. Most people thought females were always the emotional ones. Those had to be people who hadn't lived with Ten. Good heavens! She had rooms to clean, food to make, and now, possibly, a romance to patch up. She sure could use her mother's assistance or even Maria's.

The rest of the trip, technically, took ten minutes or less, but it felt like forever. A sense of what might be waiting for her rattled around in her stomach, souring the yummy lunch she'd just consumed. Mark's sedan in the parking lot both surprised and relieved her. Odd he'd be home this early. Maybe Ten called him. It wasn't unreasonable to think Ten would have. What didn't make sense was that her husband, who was on a murder case, would rush home to deal with relationship issues that would probably work themselves out in a couple of days.

The only greeting she received while entering the front door was a single bark from Jasper and a hopeful glance as his tail wagged. His bowl was empty. If things were at sixes and sevens, he may have missed a meal. "Okay, sweetie. I'll get you some food."

"Glad to hear it," Mark replied as he came through the interior door. "Some coffee would be welcomed, too. I would have started it, but with that new-fangled coffee maker of yours, I wasn't sure how to use it."

"Ha!" She doubted that. Her husband could figure out anything if he put his mind to it. "Jasper, first. Then I'll start on your coffee and food. What are you doing home so early?" She opened the fridge and removed a can of dog food, lunch meat, cheese, and a head of lettuce.

"Ten called me."

"I figured as much. I saw Sloane hanging out with tourists, but she wasn't having fun."

Mark shook his head. "I don't know anything about that. The reason Ten called was about Dalton, who is more than three sheets to the wind. Ten was afraid he might damage something."

The possibility stopped Donna in the act of opening the plastic capped dog food as she rushed over to the coffee pot. "We need to sober that man up! Did you go up and see him?"

"I did. I had to use your passkey to get in. The place is littered with bottles and smells like a dive bar." He arched his bushy eyebrows. "I'm surprised you didn't notice when you cleaned."

She held up her hand as if fending off the cleaning comment. "He always had the privacy sign on his door. I admit everyone has a right to privacy. Some of the time, those who continue to leave the sign on their door tidy up their own rooms. I'm assuming this isn't the case here."

"Nope." He grimaced. "It might be best if I took up the food and coffee."

"It would be more normal if the inn owner brought the food up." It would also be the perfect time to question the man. "Besides, you already questioned him."

"I did. Still, it was obvious he was holding something back." His hand went up to stroke his chin in his usual thinking pose. "Maybe he's drinking out of guilt. It could have been an accident."

"Broken necks are not usually accidents unless you fall down a flight of stairs and even then, they are suspect." She busied herself measuring the coffee and the water into the coffeemaker. Jasper, certain he had been forgotten, bumped into her leg. "You're next, boy. I promise."

"I can feed him," Mark volunteered.

"You could, but he likes his food a certain mixture. One-third canned food, one-third dry food, and one-third cooked rice. You have to crush up his arthritis pills and sneak them into it, too."

"This is the same dog that we've pulled gravel out of his mouth?"

"I know. He makes some impulsive decisions, but he likes what he likes. Just because you sneak him a piece of ham or a potato chip now and then doesn't mean he eats anything." Donna flipped on the coffee, then returned back to the fridge for the rice and the mayonnaise.

Mark carried a loaf of bread to the counter, along with a plate and a butter knife. "I do know how to make a sandwich. You spoil him."

Because it was true, she chose not to address the subject. "Did Dalton tell you anything interesting?"

"He misses Emily. He wishes they were still married, which I think was based on her still being alive. Rita didn't mean anything to him. It was just a fling."

"Oh," Donna drew out the word. "That explains the divorce."

"That's what I thought, too. I did read the journal that was on Emily's laptop. It was a bit confusing. She omitted names and incidents that would have been helpful. I guess she was writing only for herself. She knew all of this. The main theme was she still loved Dalton."

Donna finished preparing Jasper's food as he pranced around her feet. When she finished, she carried the dog dish to his dish mat and placed it there. Her puggle strolled up to the dish, gave it a sniff, then walked away. Oh well, maybe she'd add some meat to it later to pique his interest.

"I'm curious about the baking show contract. So far, it seems like everyone I talked to has been randomly selected. We know Marjorie was supposed to be the grandmotherly one. She wanted to be on the show to find a new husband. Bob hoped to gather publicity for his restaurant. I assume Emily and Dalton's original purpose was the same when they were originally signed up. As for Harley, I would so like for her to be the killer, but so far she hasn't struck me as intelligent enough to commit murder and not be caught red-handed."

Mark stopped in the middle of his sandwich-making to wag his index finger. "Don't be misled by her prom queen appearance. Women go around talking about how easily men are fooled by appearances. It's been my experience women can be tricked, too. If the gal is hoping to be an actress, she might be giving the performance of her life."

As much as she prided herself on her sleuthing skills, she'd defer to her husband's experience. "You're probably right. No one seems to be who or what you might think they are. The makeup woman, Mona, is not good at her job, unless she's trying to make me look bad. I can do a better job on my makeup. I have half a mind not to let her do it tomorrow."

"Remember, everyone is a source of information. People often have…"

Donna knew what he was going to say. After all, he had said it so many times, she said it along with him, "…vital facts, but they don't even realize it."

"Exactly." Mark agreed with himself, then cut the sandwich into a neat triangle. "I think a dill spear would be a nice touch along with a bag of those kettle chips. We've got to neutralize the liquor if we want to get anything out of him besides how sorry he is."

The scent of fire roasted Columbian coffee filled the room. Early on, Donna decided you couldn't run a quality inn with inferior coffee. It cost more, but she noticed in the reviews of other inns that people complained most about bad coffee and uncomfortable beds. She poured the heady brew into a white stoneware mug. "I'm not sure how I feel about serving my best blend to a possible murderer."

"I'm thinking they may have been trying to patch things up," Mark added as he withdrew the pickle jar from the fridge.

"What evidence do you have?" If they did patch things up, it would be better for their restaurant. That way they were both getting paid and could funnel the money back into the restaurant. If they had hoped for publicity, they were flat out of luck.

"I found a bra and panties in the room."

While that did raise some questions, it didn't mean it belonged to the ex-wife. "How can you be sure they were Emily's?"

Mark winked at her and plated the food. "As a veteran detective,

I do have some special observational skills. After I helped Dalton into a chair that had lingerie deposited in it, I asked him if it was his. He told me it was Emily's."

While it wasn't unusual for drunk people to lie, they usually weren't good at it. Often, they told whoppers, as in they had just arrived with the Easter Bunny. Most of their brain power was used in staying upright, or trying to walk upstairs, or heaven forbid, drive.

"I have to admit your skills are legendary. That would make it a good bet. I only read part of Emily's journal that she had open. There was nothing about the two of them and well, you know."

"Ha!" He shook a finger at her. "You knew about the journal, but did you tell me?"

Well, she hadn't, but she had meant to. "Ah, things got crazy. Baking show. Murdered contestant. My mother sneaking out of town. Sloane and Ten's on-again, off-again romance."

"Stop," Mark held up his palm to stop the flow of excuse. "No need to apologize. Wells, our expert forensic guy, uncovered the diary."

"It wasn't exactly hidden." He made it sound like it was a big deal.

He raised his brows and inhaled deeply. "It wasn't entitled important information, either. Wells dug through recipes, and files containing shoes Emily wanted to buy. That woman loved shoes, along with a book she was writing. It took a while before Wells realized it was a book. It was entitled 'What You Did Last Night.'"

Really. The woman thought that was a good title. Donna shook her head. Well, either you or Wells read the journal, I assume. What little bit I did read, it sounded like the two might get back together.

"Unlike you, I read the entire journal, and there were gaps in the dates. It wasn't a daily, dear diary kind of thing. Everything she wrote was the response of a depressed woman. Maybe she only turned to her laptop when she was bummed. If she was secretly meeting her ex, then she had no time to be typing."

"Maybe," Donna grudgingly agreed She hadn't picked up on that.

The laptop was open and on. It had gone to sleep but woke when she touched it with her glove-clad hands. Emily's room was a mess, and the computer on and opened to the journal. It meant either she was going to write in it or was reflecting back to how she felt previously. "Since everyone hot-footed it out of here so early on that morning, I didn't get to see Dalton or Emily. It would have been nice to know her state of mind."

Mark picked up the plate with the sandwich and spear and grabbed a bag of chips from the basket on the counter. "You bring the coffee. I suggest getting a thermos carafe and filling it up."

"Won't it seem odd? The two of us parading into his room?" She pulled down the carafe from the cabinet and filled it.

A hoarse chuckle came from her husband. Despite the fact he stopped smoking over a year ago, he still had the raspy, smoker laugh. "We could show up riding a circus horse, and he wouldn't blink. The important thing is to get up there before he passes out."

"This calls for desperate measures then. Let's use the elevator." She picked up the filled cup in one hand, regretting the fact she had already poured the coffee, and the carafe in the other. "Lead on. Feel free to punch the up button, too."

They moved through the hallway, not saying anything, cautious of who might overhear. Once in the elevator, Donna asked the issue that had bothered her the most about Dalton's over-imbibing. "How did he get drunk so fast? The show hasn't been over that long."

"Long enough for you to be seen at Garden Delight with today's winning contestant?"

Oh, so he *had* heard. She cut her eyes to her husband as the elevator door opened. "Jealous?"

He smirked. "Please. I know I'm the only man for you. Most people were worried that you might hurt the contestant. It's obvious your biscuits were the best. I didn't need another homicide on my hands. Besides, I would feel bad about arresting you."

They hopped out of the elevator together. State law stated that buildings open to the public had to provide elevators. It had been no easy thing to attach an elevator to her Victorian lady, either architecturally or financially. Not only did she go for the cheapest, smallest elevator, it also was the one that waited the least amount of time for passengers to dismount. Guests had to be warned not to tarry when the door opened.

"You would feel bad about it. I kind of hoped you'd let me off," she teased.

"I might be tempted, but you knew when you married me that I follow the letter of the law."

"Yeah, I know." She used her hand holding the carafe to gesture in the direction of Dalton's room. "Is the door unlocked?"

"Should be. I wouldn't expect him to be able to walk a straight line to the door and lock it. He's frat boy hung over."

"I imagine he's no serious drinker and was chugging the hard stuff. There has to be one liquor store in Legacy that's thankful for his patronage."

Restaurants, bars, and hotels were the ones to benefit the most from an influx of non-locals. Those not in the tourist industry often viewed the strangers as a nuisance without realizing they were the lifeblood of their defunct textile town.

"Yeah, maybe more than one. Odd, I don't even remember seeing him at the show. It was crazy today. Did you hear about Janice being the new judge?"

"I did. I figured you should have been a shoo-in. You can make those biscuits in your sleep."

"Yeah, me, too." They strolled over to Dalton's door and stood there as if waiting for the guest to swing the door open. "You heard about the egg incident and Harley calling me a cheater?"

"Yep." One corner of his lips tugged up into a half-smile. "I have to say you keep things from being dull around here."

It wasn't like she tried. Things just happened. "I'm glad I keep you entertained."

"Always." He reached for the doorknob and pushed the door open.

Chapter Nineteen

THE HANDSOME, GLIB Dalton she remembered from when he checked in a few days ago had been replaced by a red-eyed man with clumps of hair sticking straight out, a shirt buttoned wrong, and only one sock on. To top it off, he was listing heavily to the right, rather like a cruise liner ready to make its final tumble into the ocean.

Mark rushed in, placed the plate and chips on the table, and retrieved a pillow from the bed, which he wedged into the side of the chair. "Okay. That keeps you semi-upright. I brought you food and coffee."

A bleary-eyed Dalton blinked. "You're my ba-best friend." His eyes narrowed as he concentrated his effort. "What's your name again?"

"Mark." He picked up the sandwich and held it up to Dalton's mouth. "Take a bite for your best buddy. I made it myself."

Dalton snapped at the sandwich, taking a big bite. He chewed and talked at the same time, the much-needed food spewing everywhere. "You're the gr-gra..." He managed to spit out the desired word. "Great."

"Yeah, people tell me that all the time." Mark put the sandwich back on the plate and held out his hand for the coffee cup, which Donna gave him as he spoke. "Let's wash it down with a drink."

"I could use a drink. It helps." He grabbed onto Mark's hand that held the mug and brought it to his lips. His audible gulping made Donna glad the brew had time to cool on the way up. Finally, after emptying the mug, he blinked owlishly. "What was that? Kahlua?"

"You guessed it. How about you take a bite of the sandwich, and I'll get you some more."

Normally, if the man were sober, he would resent being talked to as if a toddler. He took another bite of sandwich, and Donna poured him more coffee and blew on it to cool it before handing it to Mark.

He held onto the cup and waited as Dalton laboriously chewed his sandwich. "What's up with all the liquor bottles in your room?"

"I need to forget. Where's my Kahlua?"

"It's cooling. We serve it hot in Legacy. Still, I wouldn't want you to burn your mouth. What are you trying to forget?" He handed Dalton the dill spear. Instead of biting it, he wiggled it. It shook and shimmied, which resulted in him giggling. The man had forgotten the question.

Donna figured it was time for her to have a go at the drunkard or grieving ex-husband, depending on what label she wanted to use. "What are you trying to forget?"

Dalton narrowed his eyes in Donna's direction. "How did you get here?"

"Elevator." She found from working with patients coming out of anesthesia, that it was best to use as few words as possible.

"Oh." He nodded his head, then grabbed it with both hands and whimpered.

"What are you trying to forget?" she repeated, since her attempt wasn't answered.

He cocked his head and grimaced. He opened and closed his mouth a couple of times without saying anything. Finally, he said,

"Are you the angel of Christmas Past?"

Donna wasn't about to correct him on the angel part. It might be the only time anyone in her life called her an angel. "Yes, I am. Any particular part of your past you want to visit?"

"I don't want to see Rita." He shook his head. "Mistake."

Mark made a point of catching her eye. She knew enough to add up Rita plus Dalton equaled divorce. She tried to make her voice soothing and somewhat angelic, although she knew that was a reach. "What are your happiest memories?"

"When I met Emily. Wait, no." He shook his head and whimpered again. "It was our wedding. Beach wedding. It was when we opened our restaurant together."

"Did you like owning a restaurant?"

Dalton's hand slipped back to rub his neck, and he glanced at the cup in Mark's hand. Without needing to be told, Mark held the cup up to the distraught man, who wrapped his hands around Mark's, lifted the hands and cup to his lips and drank deeply. He released his hands, and Mark sat the cup on the table.

So far, the angel of Christmas Past was getting nowhere. Maybe she needed another approach. "Owning a restaurant is hard work."

"Expensive." Dalton agreed. "Too expensive. Emily took another job to help." He sighed and reached for the cup.

The fact he was now manufacturing whole sentences now and then, meant he might be sobering up. Too bad. She thought she would get more out of him as the Christmas angel.

"Did someone come by and offer you a place on the baking show?"

"Yeah," he glanced up at Donna and Mark. "That's why I'm here. It was over a year ago. We jumped on it. It might be the boost Flamingoes needed."

He emptied the mug and put it down hard on the table, making Donna flinch. The glass on the tabletops was supposed to save the wood finish, but there was nothing to save the glass. So, they started picking their contestants a year ago.

"That was a while ago."

"It seems like a lifetime. Emily and I were together then. Six weeks ago, one of the guys that came by originally called up and asked if we were still on." He grimaced and gave a significant look at the empty cup. "I told him about the divorce and how things were tense between the two of us."

"That didn't discourage him?" It should have been enough for anyone with a shred of decency, but she had to remember she was talking about television. Ratings were everything. It didn't matter if it was true or would destroy a family. All that mattered was if people would watch it. She read once that the secret behind the popularity of reality shows was that people wanted to see people who were worse than them. Somehow, it made them feel better about themselves and their life.

Her husband half-turned to shoot her a look that clearly asked *who* was conducting the investigation, not the first time Donna had received such a look. She smiled and shrugged. He knew who she was when he married her. At the time, she was pretty sure he mentioned it as one of her best attributes. Then again, he may have been talking about her cooking.

Dalton slumped in the chair and stared past the two of them as he spoke. "He talked to Emily, and she was all for it, or so he told me." He exhaled audibly, then frowned. "Looking back, I think he played us against one another. Before we even arrived here, we were supposed to be all hateful to each other, but end up back in each other's arms in a tearful reunion."

The producer really knew how to play with human emotions. From what she read of the journal, Emily would have been open to the tearful reunion. What other games had he played with the contestants? Marjorie was promised enough exposure to land a new husband. She was fairly sure that Harley was told she'd land a modeling contract, be a television star, or end up as a professional sports cheerleader. The last one paid very little but left the woman open to being seen and with the possibility of marrying one of the high-earning athletes.

Bob, who went out first, thought his appearance would get publicity for his restaurant. As far as she knew, Prashant came along with Agatha in hopes of a free vacation. No one was what they seemed with the exception of herself. As far as baking, some could bluff their way through, but no one had the extreme love of baking that the British show highlighted. The show was fake from the get-go. No one walked away with any big money prize. The best they could hope for was to get their name and face out there. It certainly wasn't a reason to kill—which brought her back to who killed Emily?

"Did you know if anyone hated Emily?"

Instead of directing his answer to Donna, Dalton gazed up at Mark. "You already asked me that. I told you everyone liked her. As far as the restaurant went, she was the calm one. Even after we divorced, she still helped. Emily was half-owner and all. She never raised her voice. That was how she was. Rita was miffed when I didn't marry her once I divorced. But not so much that she didn't move on to another guy. Nope. Can't think of anyone."

That was no help. Mark pulled out a chair from the small café table she had put in the room for eating. Even still, most people missed the fact there was a table in the room and usually ate in bed, often smearing the sheets with pizza or BBQ wing sauce. While her husband probably was tired of standing, she also knew this was his two-guys talking routine, which meant she should make herself scarce. Donna refilled the coffee mug and took a few steps back, just enough to be out of general eyesight, but close enough to hear if they didn't whisper.

"Off the record, wives can be a pain, right?"

She wanted to answer that one herself but had to suck in her lips to stop herself.

"Some can," Dalton admitted. "I didn't mean to cheat on her. I drank too much, and Rita took me home."

"To your house that you shared with your wife?"

"Yes." He shook his head. "It wasn't my intention to start anything. Really! Rita started undressing me."

Donna cleared her throat, wanting to point out the obvious, but her detective husband gestured for her to leave as if she would. Instead, she motioned to locking up her lips. It would be difficult with the nonsense that was coming out of the man's mouth.

"Anyhow, Emily came home and found us," Dalton concluded and hung his head.

Before Donna could say something, Mark whistled. "You were lucky. My wife would have shot me."

"You're right about that." She couldn't stop herself from interrupting. "It wouldn't be fatal, though."

"Donna!" Her husband hissed her name.

It sounded like it was time to listen through an open door, which was at best only eighteen inches farther away. "I'm going."

Her husband waited until she left to ask the next question. "I want you to think very hard. This could be the difference between us catching your wife's killer or not. So far, I see nothing that would connect her death to the show. That means whoever killed her had a grudge against her. Can you think of anyone?"

Silence, which made her wonder if the two men were staring at one another or if Dalton was trying to kick his alcohol-laden memory into gear.

"Emily was always so sweet and nice to everyone. She was one of the most popular girls in high school. Maybe the most popular. That's why I was so surprised she went out with me. I wasn't the quarterback or the rich kid with the Porsche. For Pete's sake, she was not only the homecoming queen, but the prom queen, too."

Donna had her ear angled toward the few inches she had with the door cracked open. Probably dozens of girls had hated Emily, although the two had been out of high school probably ten years or more. That would have been a long time to hold onto a grudge. It seemed a very thin thread to hang a motivation on. Still, people had killed for lesser reasons.

Her husband cleared his throat. Sometimes, that meant he was going for the big question. Other times, it was just a throat clearing. "So, Dalton, can't you think of anyone who was really irritated with Emily?"

"Well," he started, then stopped.

"Go on," Mark encouraged. "Anything could help."

"I was dating this weird chick when I met Emily. When I dropped her, she threatened me. Her goal was to be a navy seal before they were even letting women into the program. She was freakishly strong. Some of the guys used to call her Man Arms."

It sounded possible that Man Arms could be unstable and a class A grudge holder.

The bell on the door jingled as people stomped into the inn, talking and laughing. Good heavens! What did people think the inn was? Oh yeah, it was a place where people could come and go as they pleased, part of the B and B deal. Unfortunately, she missed the name of the possible killer.

Chapter Twenty

T HE SOUND OF feet coming up the stairs had Donna backing away. It wouldn't look good to be hovering so close to Dalton's door. Guests might think she was eavesdropping or even worse, peeking. The last thing The Painted Lady Inn needed was a creepy reputation. With only seven available rooms to rent, most of the time she barely broke even. The plans to use the front parlor and dining room for receptions put a little extra money in her pocket, along with the mother and daughter teas.

While out of state guests usually booked the rooms, the real money was in the locals who wanted to use the inn for everything from staged photos and tea parties to receptions. The average citizen didn't mind shelling out money as long as it excused them from cleaning up. On the upside, she didn't have to change sheets for those events.

As the steps came closer, she busied herself in the small sitting area that was on every floor. A small sink, fridge, and microwave backed up to a plumbing wall. The room on the other side might occasionally get the hum of the microwave through their bathroom wall, but no one had commented on it so far.

She wet the dish towel she had tucked into her apron and wiped off the counter. No reason to pretend. The nook certainly needed the cleaning help. She chased the large crumbs around with her cloth, finally corralling them.

"There you are," Ten announced, causing Donna to turn. "I've been looking for…" He coughed, then made a guttural groan sounding a bit like an engine that wouldn't catch before pushing out the words "…for Mark or you. I saw your cars in the parking lot."

It wasn't a guest, which made her wonder what happened to all the other voices. That significant pause let her know all was not well in Ten's world. It didn't take an iota of her deductive skills due to the fact she'd seen a crying Sloane earlier, hanging out in an itsy, bitsy bikini. It wasn't the way Donna would have dealt with heartache, but to each his own. She also noticed Ten had hoped to find Mark and not her. It made sense. She wasn't exactly an expert on dealing with women, despite being one.

"Mark's in with Dalton." She hesitated in saying anymore. Ten couldn't be classified as a gossip, but he wasn't careful about whom he shared information with. At one time, his loose lips had frat boys crawling through her basement windows as part of an initiation rite. They must have assumed, after all of Ten's stories, that they had a fifty percent chance of dying or meeting the spirit of someone who had died in the inn. So far, she hadn't encountered any.

Her husband's location didn't please her employee. He sucked in a long exhale, then let it go in a dramatic sigh. "Okay, I guess you'll do."

"I'm flattered."

"You're not known for your warm and fuzzy advice."

"Not surprised. I'm more surprised that Mark is, though."

Ten cocked his head to one side as he considered her words. "It's not that the advice is that different. It's the way you deliver it. Mark puts it out there as a suggestion you can take or reject. You're more like I gave you good advice, now run with it."

"Come on." She wasn't like that. She placed the towel on the sink rim while making a mental note not to leave it there. With all the camera phone owners in the inn, someone would take a picture of the cloth, post it, and call it unsanitary. As a former nurse, she'd put the inn's cleanliness up against any other B and B or chain hotel. "Spill it."

On second thought, that probably wasn't the best way to handle a distraught male. Besides love issues, he was probably dealing with transition fears to the next stage of his life.

"I realize this must be a difficult time for you with so many changes in your life. What seems to be bothering you today?"

Ten grimaced. "That's worse. You sound like one of those fake doctors on television who have their own shows. They pretend to care as long as the camera's rolling."

Was he saying she didn't care? Both hands fisted on her hips. "I care. I wouldn't have put up with some of your antics for so long if I didn't."

A small chuckle sounded as he wrinkled his nose. "There's the Donna I know and trust. Sloane broke up with me."

"Pardon me?" Obviously, she misheard, especially after Ten had made a grand gesture of cooking lunch for his sweetie. They had even scheduled all their get-togethers for the next twelve months.

"You heard me. Sloane's mother didn't think it was fair to me or her to have a long-distance relationship. Personally, I think she was worried mainly about herself. While she tolerated me, I always had the feeling I wasn't good enough for her daughter. What's your advice? Lay it on me without the phony therapist talk."

He was asking for her advice. Normally, she would have plenty to say. The problem with advice was when it didn't work the way it should, people tend to blame whomever gave the advice. In this case, it would be her. Donna had no intentions of climbing into that mud pit. However, she'd give him something to work with. Sometimes, she just couldn't help herself. "Tennyson…"

"You're using my full name." He gave a little moan and put his head in his hands.

"Remember, you're an adult, which makes sense that I would use your name. People at your new job will use it, so get ready. Part of being an adult is making hard decisions. Sloane is an adult, too. I'm all for children respecting their parents, but I wouldn't expect Sloane's mother to know what's right for her daughter. She might *think* she does base on her own experiences, but mothers and daughters are never the same. The two of you need to decide what's best for you, not Sloane's mother."

Ten lowered his hands revealing his surprised expression, then he slowly shook his head. "I had no clue what you might say, but that wasn't it. Even better, it makes sense. What if your advice has always made sense, but I had to grow up to realize it?"

"Sounds about right to me." At last, he was realizing her wisdom. Maybe she would have made a good parent.

"It would." He patted her arm as he turned toward the stairs. "I need to call Sloane."

Did he have a sudden epiphany that all her advice was great, or was he humoring her, knowing that he'd be gone in a few weeks?

Dalton's door opened as Mark exited. Whatever the guests were doing downstairs would have to wait. Donna snagged the towel she didn't want to forget and hustled over to Mark.

"Well? Do you know the name of Man Arms?"

He shook his head. "Nope. She was just weird and not the love of his life. He didn't bother remembering her name. It's a false lead. If there was such a woman around here, I suspect she'd kill Dalton, instead."

"There you go, showing you know nothing about women, especially those with a few loose screws."

He gestured to the stairs. Donna knew what he was asking. Since she had no real reason to use the elevator, she strolled to the stairs with her husband. Going down wasn't that bad with gravity assisting with every step as if it wanted her on a lower level.

Donna tucked her arm into Mark's, not so much out of affection, but to keep him close as they spoke. So much of their conversation could be misinterpreted, and the inn would end with an *ick* factor due to their conversations usually involving murder.

"Women who obsess on a guy, for whatever reason, want him to be their hero. If he has flaws, they overlook them. If he has the bad taste to pick another girl over them, they transfer their anger onto the girl."

"It takes two to tangle. Besides, Dalton left that female a good decade ago."

Her attempt to discover Man Arms might be a waste of her energy. Still, so far, it was as close to a lead as they had. "That means she's had that long into making him into something he's not in her mind. He's divorced, which shows he's realized the error of his ways or the spell Emily put on him finally wore off."

"Okay, I'll give you that. Why hasn't she approached Dalton yet? She should get in before the man finds himself married again."

Their steps were matched as they slowly descended the staircase. Voices drifted up from the second-floor parlor, along with the canned laughter from a sitcom. That answered where her guests went. She needed to get to work on her snack smorgasbord as soon as she finished picking her husband's brain. Her left hand trailed along the smooth banister, not that she needed it for support. She just liked touching it. Every little nuance about the inn made her heart sing. Still, she had a murder to solve.

"How do we know he *hasn't* met his old girlfriend? I'm sure she's changed. Could even be disguised. He really doesn't remember anything significant about her, which would make her hard to track. How would we identify her?"

Mark cleared his throat and hummed a little. "Good question. I would say anyone who was exceptionally friendly to him."

The suggestion made Donna snort. For a great detective, he sometimes missed the obvious. Thank goodness he had her on his team. "He's a good looking, single man in a Southern town. What woman is not going to be nice to him? A few might think he could make tons of money being on the show. There are plenty of mothers looking to play matchmaker for their daughters. It might be easier to find a woman who hasn't been nice to him."

"There's you."

Donna lifted her hand off the banister to pinch her husband's arm.

"Ow! That hurt."

"It should." She elbowed him with the arm still hooked into his when they reached the landing. "What you said hurt me. I work very hard to be civil to everyone who walks through The Painted Lady Inn's doors."

He chuckled, which caused Donna to send him a dark look. Good thing Ten didn't come to her husband for romantic advice. He might have told him to ridicule Sloane.

"Sweetie." Mark unhooked their locked arms to wrap his arms around her in a tight hug. "I never said you were mean to him. What I meant was you were probably the only female over ten who wasn't flirting with him."

"Oh." That she could accept as Mark dropped his arms and

stepped back. Most Southern women were proficient at the gentle art of wrapping men around their finger before they entered primary school. Even though her mother may have tried to pass on the skills, Donna had no desire in pretending interest she didn't have or in offering compliments that weren't merited, which was probably why she ended up paying full price for car repairs.

"I can accept that. As for the case, maybe we should talk in the kitchen while I whip up some snacks."

"That sounds great." Enthusiasm colored his words, which equated to him missing lunch.

"It's not for you. It's for the guests. I think it's the least I can do since they keep missing breakfast."

"I gave vouchers to the ones who were up at a normal time. It wouldn't have helped the early risers since no restaurant opens before nine." He wiggled his shaggy brows. "The Sunrise Café should feel some guilt naming themselves that. They don't open until well after dawn."

"If you're trying to make me feel better, you're not succeeding. I only feel worse that all those involved in the show have had to survive on bad coffee and stale donuts from that gas station along the highway."

The two of them made their way through the hallway and into the kitchen without being spotted by any guests. Once inside the inner sanctum, as Mark liked to refer to the kitchen, he headed for the coffee maker. He pulled out the empty carafe and held it up. "I've been robbed. I had to watch Dalton drink cup after cup of delicious joe. Here I was inhaling the robust scent and thinking soon I will have my fingers around a cup. Now, this!"

"Don't be so dramatic. Maybe you should be on the baking show because so far it seems to me like everyone is acting a part. No one seems to be who you think they are." She picked her way to the freezer to retrieve the coffee grounds. Her puggle didn't make it easy as he weaved in between her feet. "I'll make some more coffee. You can get the cups out."

"I can do that." He went to the cabinet and withdrew two white, stoneware cups. "I can't understand anyone wanting to kill Emily. I would have to say even Rita is out. Dalton would recognize her, which ends up with grasping straws and playing with the idea someone could be holding a grudge for over a decade."

Those who worked in law enforcement expected logical motivations. If he bothered to really pay attention to her police dramas, then he'd know murderers were seldom logical. His excuse for not watching was he already saw enough of it at work. He didn't need anymore. "Hatfield and McCoy's feud. I heard that no one even remembered what they were fighting about."

"You got me on that one. Still, that's an unusual example."

Donna filled the coffee pot, flipped it on, and hustled over to the oven to start it for the first round of appetizers. "There are plenty of families who don't talk ever due to something stupid and usually trivial one of the members did."

"I agree that people get out of sorts over not getting Grandmother's Desert Rose china pattern. This isn't Great Aunt Hilda's pearls, either. We have a dead body in the morgue I can't release yet, just in case it gives us more clues."

Even though she had seen her share of dead bodies, going down to see another one didn't appeal. She pulled the labeled appetizers out of the freezer and placed them on the counter. "Did the medical examiner tell you anything?"

"We couldn't lift any fingerprints from the neck. There was a tiny bit of latex residue found which means the killer took time to don some latex gloves. There were bruises that the medical examiner concluded were made by fingers. Now, I can see a crime of passion when another person attacks a rival. The gloves scream pre-meditated. It had to be someone who followed Emily here. The female wasn't here long enough to stir up hate and discord among the residents."

"I expected the premediated part. Someone could shoot some-one or even stab them on the spur of the moment. No one snaps a person's neck because they tripped and then reached for the person's neck to hold them up. It was planned."

"Do you think it has anything to do with the show?"

"Yes and no. As you know, I nosed around and found out some of the contestants were promised five hundred dollars a day. It isn't chicken feed, but I haven't heard of anyone being paid yet. Greed can't be much of a motive. Still, there had to be some type of advanced promotion showing our killer where he or she might find Emily, if she was the target. There's also the possibility that she just got in the way."

Mark's phone chimed while he poured himself coffee. "I don't want to know. It's always something."

Most people would expect a picturesque town like Legacy to be crime free, but it wasn't. She picked up the phone he had placed on the island and answered it. "Mark Taber's Answering Service." Then she handed it to him.

She already knew it was work, she might as well find a to-go cup. Even though it went against her quality food principles, she'd nuke some appetizers. That way he'd have something to eat.

He ended the call. "The test kitchen has been vandalized. I'll be surprised if you have a show to go to tomorrow."

Chapter Twenty-One

THE ENTIRE BEDROOM was bathed in gray shadows, not quite six, that much Donna knew. Her alarm would have gone off, and today would have started like the past two days with her rushing to the set. This time, she wouldn't make the mistake of showing up late and getting chewed on by Mona, the makeup girl. She certainly was an odd one. The woman, who was shaken up from finding Emily dead, was totally different from the woman who did makeup badly. Sometimes, she gave good advice, and other times, she just fussed about Donna being late.

As peculiar as she might be, Mona couldn't hold a candle to the husband of one of her anniversary couples. When Donna had placed all the nibbles out for everyone, David made a point of asking where Mark was. That in itself was odd. He had no real reason to know her husband except for a few flashes of him in the inn. Donna was fairly certain she hadn't introduced them.

Ten, who must have a police scanner in his room, told Mr. Busy Body that Mark was probably at the vandalized test kitchen. There was nothing funny about the remark, yet the man roared when he heard about it, enough that his wife tried to calm him down.

When a guest was this odd or rude, the best she could do was wish them gone. This couple had stayed longer than most. Legacy did have a run of good weather that would make beach walking or shelling pleasant, but as far as she could tell, the couple had never hit the beach. Most beachgoers returned, bringing in enough sand to create another beach. No one went to the beach this week, or the guests they had visiting hadn't.

The light around the blinds brightened, and the clock radio gave its final click before the clock radio roared to life. "It's another beautiful day! Someone must be living right. The high today will only be 82."

Her husband rolled over with a grunt, taking most of the covers with him. She could accept he wasn't a morning person. As a nurse who had worked first shift for most of her thirty-plus years career, she'd had no choice. It transitioned well into owning a B and B, since she had to be up before the guests to fix breakfast. Time to get the day started. She swung her feet out of bed when Mark muttered something.

"What?"

Mark pulled down the covers to speak. "The medical examiner found nine finger marks on Emily's neck, which I thought was weird because, as you know, most of us have ten fingers."

"Not everyone," she reminded him. "We have plenty of farmers who are missing a digit or two. I imagine there are some soldiers missing a finger, too. Should I be on the lookout for a nine-fingered man?"

"Or woman," her husband responded.

"I will look for both," she agreed and tried to remember David's hands. He was a big man with big hands that would have easily fit around Emily's neck. His wife had mentioned something about him being in the Green Berets, too. "I'll get dressed in the bathroom and start the coffee before I leave."

"You're a saint!" Mark called out from his cushy location on the bed.

"I know. Before you ask, yes, we are still filming. Mona made a point to call me and tell me, probably because I'm always late."

"I'll see if I can drop by to see you crowned Baker Extraordinaire."

He was teasing, and she gave it right back. "Of course, I should win *if* there is any fairness in the world. Maybe I'll let you buy me lunch."

"I'll be there. Did you want to take some food today for the crew?"

She had almost forgotten. There would be those who would think she was bribing the others with food. Far from that. She wanted to show them she had range. Donna Tollhouse Taber wasn't just *any* baker. The same way she wasn't just a former nurse or a current B and B owner.

"Thanks. Mona can earn her pay today. I don't have time for makeup."

It took her a little less than twenty minutes to load up the car with yummies and drive to the test kitchen. At the site, the lights were on, people were milling, and the chairs were set up for the audience. It was hard to say what had been vandalized. When she drew closer to the kitchen area, which was all painted in white, she could see that some of the white paint was a different texture, more of a gloss that would catch the light every time a camera was used. Whoever thought this was an answer to what she assumed were some ugly words should have taken a painting course at the local hardware store.

Whenever something bad happened like this, people usually blamed it on out-of-towners or teens from the next town over. She wasn't sure why, but those children were always the likely culprits. Harley was exiting the makeup trailer, or she thought it was Harley.

It was the right height and the appropriate amount of attitude. Instead of sexy, country girl, *it* was scary vampire today with a white face, heavily outlined eyes, and a blood red slash of a mouth. *It* almost made her afraid to enter the trailer.

The producer wanted conflict so constantly changed things. It was hard to say if Harley's varied wardrobe was her idea or the producer's. Didn't he realize people needed someone they could like and cheer in the show? The inoffensive Bob was gone, but maybe he wasn't. She remembered in an Agatha Christie novel where the murderer was the first person who supposedly died. Of course, in Bob's case, the first one eliminated.

Donna breezed in without knocking. "Are you ready for me?"

The woman shot her a look that was less than inviting. "I didn't expect you to be on time. I was going to take a smoke break."

She could do without nicotine hands on her face. "I think I'm the last one. You can whip through my makeup and take your break. Make it extra-long. Did you also do the men's makeup?"

This might be her last chance to pry information out of Mona. Donna knew she was a substitute baker and wasn't supposed to win. Therefore, it would make sense if she was cut today leaving Marjorie, Prashant, and Queen of the Night to battle it out.

"The Emcee, Justin, brought his own makeup guy. The producer, Claude, decided if he was paying for a makeup artist for Justin, he could do the other men on the set, too. The way the men are dropping, there will only be Justin left while I have just as many faces to fix as I always did."

While Donna didn't appreciate the expression *faces to fix*, she decided not to mention it. Mona was already in a snit over not having any of her people kicked out of the running. The best she could do was change the conversation. It was obvious the woman worked out. "I bet you're staying down at the chain hotel on the highway with the workout room."

Mona, who had been moving stuff around on her tray glanced up, meeting Donna's eyes in the mirror. "I am. Why would you assume that?"

Most people answered nosy questions without too much fuss, but there was always that one person. "I couldn't help noticing how buff you are. I think it's great you work out."

"Uh-huh." Her response lacked any conviction. "That's not what I usually hear. Most men call me a freak, and a few women do, too." She pushed up a sleeve and made an impressive bicep. "This body got me into the navy seals program. They were just experimenting with letting women in to see if they had what it takes."

"It must have been exciting to be the first." Even though she worked hard to keep her tone matter of fact, her mental machinations went into overdrive. Women who wanted to be navy seals weren't thick on the ground. In fact, no female had graduated, so far. What were the chances that the woman behind her wasn't Dalton's ex-girlfriend? Forget the math. Her stomach flipflopped the way it always did when she found herself in a pickle.

No need to mention the obvious, that the woman could break Donna like a toothpick or even the much smaller Emily. Why would Emily have any reason to be afraid of the makeup artist? Mark called her out for jumping to conclusions more than once, but she was ninety-nine percent sure she was in the presence of Emily's murderer. Best thing to do was test her reaction to her beloved's name. "Shame about Dalton being cut."

The reflection blinked, then her lips firmed. "Yeah, it is a shame. The guy didn't have what it takes. Not enough drama. Not like you. You're drama, drama, drama!"

Having worked in the hospital for what seemed forever, Donna knew the snap of latex gloves. She'd donned plenty of them and recognized the sound. What she didn't expect was to see Mona putting on gloves. "Why the gloves?"

"I always wear them."

The woman must have a different definition of always than she did. "You didn't wear them yesterday."

"Should have." Mona bobbed her head. "Strange as it may seem, I am highly allergic to the makeup."

Donna watched her wrestle her pinky finger into the glove. As if feeling her eyes on her, Mona flourished her hand. "That did me in with the seals. Broke my hand in a training exercise. I wasn't good enough anymore, because I lacked some mobility in my hand. If the navy doc was any good, he would have fixed my hand. Still, I'm plenty strong."

It must have infuriated Mona that Emily didn't recognize her. When you spend a good part of your life resenting someone, that person should acknowledge you.

Donna slumped in her seat as Mona turned to face her. "Sit up. I can't work on anyone who's slumping."

In other words, it was hard to strangle someone whose neck wasn't within easy reach, not that Donna intended to be. She looked up at Mona towering over her and pretended compliance as she lowered one foot to the floor. On the counter, in front of the mirror sat a curling iron. The red glowing light meant it was on. All she had to do was get from here to outside where everyone was.

In between her and freedom was Mona, who had already donned latex gloves. Maybe it was more than a badly healed hand that got her kicked out the seals program. Seals had to be mentally tough.

Her hand slid into the pocket of her shirt. On a less busy day, she would have picked something other than the gingham shirt with contrasting pockets. It was so grandmotherly, but she needed pockets for her phone and keys.

Mark was the number two on her speed dial. All she had to do was dial him, keep Mona talking, and not get killed in the process. "I'm trying to sit up, but I'm so tired. Dalton wanted to stay up all night and tell everyone about his high school years."

"He did?" She handed Donna a baby wipe.

The usual drill was for her to run it across her face to remove any makeup she had on. It took some thought, but she did it with her left hand while keeping her eyes on Mona's reflection in the mirror. "Oh, yes. He seemed to be nostalgic. Not sure if I told you, he was staying at my inn."

"Oh, so that's where he's at." A gleam sparked in her eyes.

Donna hoped Dalton was taking a fast plane home for his sake. "He mentioned a girlfriend."

"Emily," the angry reflection snarled the name. "It always has been Emily, the perfect."

Makeup girl had gone from menacing to psychotic in five seconds flat. Donna needed to stay calm enough to get a confession. More importantly, Mona had to bring it down a few notches before she had another murder to her name. *Breathe in. Breathe out.* Maintain a bored expression. Killers could be like animals who attacked when they sensed fear. Part of her brain wanted to tell her killers were nothing like animals. Right now, she needed to stall, until she got a confession or death appeared imminent.

"No, that wasn't the name. I understood he was married to Emily, but he definitely wasn't talking about her. Someone he knew *before* Emily. He said something about he should never have let her go. There is a mystery woman in his past."

The woman in the mirror picked up a strip of fabric, possibly a scarf. She tightened it in her hands and asked, "What was her name?"

The fabric ripped in half from the tension put on it. If Mona wanted to be undercover for her job on the show, there was a good chance she'd changed her name. Most of the time, when people changed their names, they make sure it was nothing like their former name. "Her name was—" Donna paused, not sure what to say. When in doubt, go with the truth. "One of the guests wanted something, so I never heard her name."

The torn fabric fluttered to the floor. Mona turned her back to the mirror to root around in her supply box. Now would be the perfect time to escape. She probably had about a ten percent chance of not being tackled in the process. Just in case Mark thought this was an accidental purse dial, she raised her voice enough to carry.

"What did you have against Emily? She seemed a sad, pathetic woman who didn't even get to be in the show."

"Ha!" A harsh chuckle sounded as Mona pivoted toward the mirror with a pair of scissors in her hands. "Shows what you know. Emily was one of *those* girls."

Donna's eyebrows went up as she spotted movement outside of the slightly ajar trailer door. She obviously hadn't closed it all the way, or maybe someone had opened it. Fortunately, Mona took Donna's raised eyebrows as a response to her statement.

"I guess you don't know about *those* girls because you were probably one, born into wealthy, powerful families. Because they had attractive parents, they end up with that cool, ice princess look that dares every boy to try to warm them up."

"That was so *not* me." It may not have been the right time to say something, but if she was going to be stabbed with scissors, she would rather it be for being an amateur sleuth who sometimes took chances than to be mistaken for a former ice princess. That would be so unfair. "Did Emily recognize you?"

"No!" Mona stepped behind the chair and gripped the back of it. Her hands were so close to Donna's head that it was hard not to wonder about the scissors, but Mona kept talking. "I gave her hints. Asked about high school. She didn't want to talk. The snob wouldn't even meet my eyes in the mirror. She thought she was so much better than me!"

The hot, angry words ruffled Donna's hair. She'd have to do something to send her over the edge, which might provide an opening. She eyed the hot curling iron as she plotted her escape.

Donna had both feet on the floor, and her body was stretched out extra-long across the bottom portion of the chair, keeping her vulnerable neck out of reach. "So, why did you kill your rival?" She dropped to the floor, rolled right, grabbed the cord of the curling iron, and pulled it to her, burning herself in the process. "Ouch!"

"You knew!" Mona advanced, flourishing her scissors in her right hand. "I enjoyed killing Emily, but I'm going to enjoy killing you more."

"Think of Dalton." Donna steadied herself against the wall with her left hand as she slid up to a crouching position. Normally, she didn't credit the physical toll of running a bed and breakfast for more than exhaustion and working up an appetite, but it did give her plenty of practice squatting as she cleaned under beds. She hid the curling iron down by her right side which was turned away from Mona. Curling irons never held onto their heat once unplugged, which meant she had to act *now*. Shouting outside the trailer distracted Mona for the briefest moment, just long enough for

Donna to surge to her feet and whack Mona's right forearm with the hot iron, causing her to drop the scissors.

"Why you!" Mona reached both glove-clad hands for Donna, but she was no longer there. Instead, the baker turned sleuth was on all fours and crawling with the same enthusiasm as a baby who had spotted an unguarded cup. In Donna's case, it was the door, which swung open.

Clipboard Girl Tori had her hand on it, but she was speaking to someone behind her. "This is the makeup trailer. I'm not sure what you think is going on."

Before she could say another word, Mona leaped and knocked down Tori in the process, giving Donna enough time to scamper around the entangled two. The trailing foot of her would-be killer gave her a good kick in the ribs, but it didn't slow her down, especially when she spotted Mark, Dalton, and her second favorite cop, Officer Wells, standing a few feet ahead. *Sanctuary.*

She ran to Mark's open arms.

"Donna, are you okay?"

"I am now," she mumbled into his shirt.

While she could congratulate herself on her fast thinking, she always felt safe inside her husband's arms. He'd probably tell her she should have left immediately at the first whiff of suspicion. That type of behavior was for amateurs, which she wasn't. This would be the tenth murder she'd helped to solve, and it needed solving. She pushed out of her husband's arms only to see Officer Wells taking advantage of the downed murderer to snap on the handcuffs.

Dalton turned to Mark. "I'm not sure I know her."

"Yes, you do." Donna felt the need to point out the obvious. "She told me all about your romance and how you dropped her cold for Emily."

"You're saying that woman killed Emily?" Dalton blinked as if having difficulty processing the possibility.

"She did. Told me as much, along with several interesting tidbits such as she was drummed out of the navy seals training program."

"Yeah. Man Arms always wanted to be a navy seal or a green beret." His gaze followed Officer Wells as he escorted the woman through the crowd. Another officer joined him, which was a good thing. Mona was not going easily. A few snarled curses carried on the wind. There was an occasional mention of Donna's name, too.

Mark wrapped his arm around her in a half-embrace. "I bet you're ready to go home."

The director, a middle-aged man sporting a comb-over and a spray-on tan, waved frantically at them. "What's the hold-up?"

Hollywood people. Donna rolled her eyes as the man moved closer. Her husband, usually the soul of discretion, waited until the man was close enough, revealing bloodshot eyes, indicative of allergies or more likely a flirtation with the bottle. "Any more contestants killed?" he asked very matter-of-factly.

"None," Mark answered just as coolly. "You lost your makeup artist."

Before Mark could explain the nature of the loss, the producer interrupted, "Which one?"

"Mona."

Once again, the man rudely cut Mark off. "I'm grateful for little miracles. If it was Phillip, Justin's guy, that would have killed the show." He glanced at Donna. "You're a mess. Go see Phillip, he's in the turquoise trailer. Tell him to give you the works because you're the star now."

Stunned, Donna stared open-mouthed at the man. Her sweetie had no issues responding.

"Are you out of your mind? Donna managed to fight off Mona and emerge alive, which was more than Emily could do, and you want to go on with the show? It's a crime scene." He dropped his arm from around Donna to stab his index finger emphatically at the man who showed as much heart as a rock.

The producer, Claude, cocked his head and grinned. "Technically, the show isn't a crime scene. Mona's trailer is. Besides, all the participants are alive. I used to work on a crime drama." He gave a superior nod. "I know these things."

Even though Donna had a love of crime dramas, Mark didn't. He inhaled deeply, probably trying to control his temper with those involved in crime dramas who thought they knew everything about police work. More than once she had to listened to his rant that if every police department had such fancy equipment, they could solve crimes within sixty minutes, too.

"Uh-huh. I am sure you do. We need to secure the trailer and wherever she's staying."

Claude, the producer, glared at Tori, who was still on the ground. "Get the detective the information he needs." He turned to Donna and a wide, fake smile stretched his lips wide. "Now, you need to scoot. Stardom awaits."

Donna sucked her lips in. Going home and going to bed sounded tempting, but so did baker stardom. There might be a few things she still needed to snoop into, such as what if Mona wasn't working alone. The only way she could do that was if she was in the show.

Epilogue

MAJESTIC MUSIC FILLED the second parlor as a huge American flag waved in the wind on the sixty-five-inch television screen. The words *America's Best Bakers* scrolled across the screen. Janice hurried into the room, clutching a champagne glass and a plate crowded with appetizers.

"Don't start it without me!"

"No worries," Donna assured her friend and scooted over on the sectional unit to make room for her, which forced her mother to wiggle a little closer to Maria. "We're still on the closeup of the flag that must have lasted a minute so far."

The scene cut to Justin, the emcee, sounding like a game show host, which is what he had been until his show *Who Gives Up* was canceled. Apparently, the audience was the first to give up.

Her mother reached for her hand and squeezed it. "I'm so glad you have the shows on DVD so we can watch them. I'm sorry I wasn't here."

"No worries. I suspect you were having a better time than I was."

Her mother laughed, earning a reproving look from Janice. Apparently, her friend was taking the watching of the show much too seriously. Donna pushed the pause on the remote. "You weren't even in the first show."

"I was in the audience. They might do an audience pan."

"Fair," she agreed and started the show again. They sat and

watched the six shows, which only took a little under three hours with no commercials. Even though she wouldn't admit it to friends or family, Donna had watched the show several times already. She especially liked the part where Justin pinned a blue ribbon on her harvest cake that she renamed May Day cake and had used apricot filling instead of pumpkin. Then he called her in his resonant announcer voice *The Best Baker in America*. While she knew it was far from the truth, it still appealed after hearing it a half-dozen times.

After the final credits rolled by, Janice was the first to comment.

"Did you notice they cut out everything I said about The Croaking Frog? The whole point of being a judge was to drum up publicity for my restaurant. It's not like they paid me."

"True," Donna concurred. No money had reached her, either. The producer was kind enough to send her the finished DVDs. He told her they were shopping the show around, hoping some network would be interested. "As far as I can tell, no one got to mention their restaurant or inn. They even cut Marjorie's long padded bio and her qualifications for a husband. It's a bare-bones project."

Maria sniffed from her end of the couch. "I hear they're in legal trouble."

While Cecilia handled local gossip, Maria had her finger on the pulse of everything that happened outside of Legacy.

The fact Donna hadn't heard this until now surprised her. "Why is that?"

"There's been some push back from the British show this is loosely based on. Some noise about intellectual property infringement."

"Maybe," Donna was forced to agree. "They said America as many times as they could. What specifically did they have a problem with?"

"The British judge, or should I say, the judge with a phony accent? Didn't she have family problems, too?"

A family problem was a euphemism Claude, the producer, used whenever someone vanished from the show. "Well, she didn't die, if that is what you mean. Agatha must have caught wind that the cast of the British show was coming for a look-see. She staged her own poisoning by eating arsenic. She'd hoped that would scare Claude enough to let her out of her contract. Being Claude, he was determined to roll with it no matter what. Apparently, his former partner, David, the male of the couple who would not leave, was the one who notified the British show that they were being ripped off."

Cecilia worked herself up to the edge of her seat with a few wiggles and twists, then asked, "Will anything come of it? Aren't most of the shows out there pretty much the same?"

"Most of them are," Janice concurred, "especially if one hits big. A ton of copycat shows follow. None are ever as good as the original hit. I doubt anything will come of the legal suit."

An abundance of noise outside made Donna curious. The men had decided to bypass the show, even Mark, which stung a little. What could be so important that her own husband couldn't sit beside her and watch her be named *America's Best Baker* for the seventh time? Eighth, if she included the actual event. She heard something fall out on the porch, then a shout. Janice's hand landed on her arm before she could stand.

"Donna, didn't you tell me your guest was behind the vandalism?"

"That was David, the used-to-be partner. I'm not sure when the two of them split ways. He must not be the sharpest knife in the drawer. He left the spray cans he used to vandalize the test kitchen in the bedroom trashcan." Donna blew out through her teeth in disbelief. "This with a cop in the house. Mark decided to talk to him about the vandalism. He claimed that he and Claude had different artistic views on how the show should play out. Claude wanted it to be a replica of the British show with a much smaller budget while David wanted it to be a parody. Kinda like those songs Weird Al Yankovic does. It would explain the contestants. In the end, it felt like Claude was going for parody, too, although he claimed everything had a deeper meaning. Every time Harley showed up in an even more bizarre outfit, he claimed she was showing a different facet of her personality."

Mark entered the room and signaled to Janice, which in itself was weird. Donna watched her friend leave, wondering what was up. No birthdays this month, no special conferences she knew about. The baking show was it. The crew had packed up and left, leaving patches of dead grass in the common area and a murderer in the jail awaiting her hearing. Even the town's brief brush with television was fading due to talk about changes in the Mrs. North Carolina Pageant. Rumors abounded about shapewear being worn and tattoos covered with concealer and powder.

Donna's one shining moment was now an afterthought in the town's collective mind. In a year, only she, Mark, Dalton, and a certain makeup artist would remember it. Her mother stood, gave a little wave, "I need to hit the little girl's room."

Had everyone turned into pod people? As far as Donna could remember, she had been brought up never to mention bodily functions, such as going to the restroom. A lady simply left or was indisposed. Her mother never ever *hit* the little girl's room. She cut her eyes to Maria, looking for that tell-tale sign that she wasn't who she thought she was.

Her sister-in-law gave her a sympathetic smile. "I did warn Mark you were too good of a sleuth to put anything past you."

"I am." Why didn't she know what they were trying to put past her? The song associated with the show roared into existence outside with a few missed notes. Maria stood and held out her hand.

"I was told to bring you out the side door, so you can get the full effect."

As much as she wanted to ask the full effect of what, she didn't. A world class sleuth should know. Donna allowed her sister-in-law to lead her through the inn with Jasper following. She held the door open for her pooch as they walked outside. The music was much louder once she exited. It had to be Legacy's High School Marching Band. What they may have lacked in talent, they more than made up for in enthusiasm.

As she came around the inn, she noticed the banner stretched across the verandah. *America's Best Baker Lives Here.* There was a small podium on the porch along with a sound system, a couple of potted palms, and her husband standing next to the mayor.

Mark picked up the microphone. "Here she comes ladies and gentlemen, boys and girls, bakers and non-bakers, alike. The pride of Legacy's culinary world and my wife, I am very pleased to say." He patted his stomach, causing laughter to ripple throughout the group that had gathered on her lawn.

Mark motioned for her to join him on the podium. Donna hissed to her companion. "Why didn't you tell me to doll up?"

"I tried. I believe your words were that you were off makeup due to almost dying in the makeup chair."

She did say that or something close to it. "If something like this happens again, just tell me and I will pretend to be surprised."

Donna mounted the steps of her own inn and turned to see

hundreds of people cheering for her. If anyone asked her, she'd be surprised if that many people knew her name. She saw some of her former co-workers near the front. There was Officer Wells and his family. Most of Maria's family and friends were there. Sloane was near the edge of the porch waving her left hand that would shoot a spark of light now and then, a testimony of if young people were left to their own devices, they usually figured things out.

The mayor presented her with the key to the city and officially declared May 5th to be Donna Tollhouse Taber day, dedicated to one of the city's most colorful citizens. The term *colorful*—usually the term applied to a peculiar relative—grated a bit and was often followed by *bless your heart*.

Even though she knew a speech was expected, her mind went blank as her hand tightened around the microphone. It would have been nice to have had a heads up, but she hadn't.

Mark gave her an encouraging smile and mouthed, "I love you."

She should have expected he was up to something. Even though it had been a slapped together production, Donna still enjoyed her part—not the almost being killed, but the baking part. If no one else knew, at least the folks in Legacy would know she gave it her all. She held the mike up to her face.

"I am thankful for each one of you. Every person in this town has taken a turn at weaving the tapestry that is Legacy. I appreciate the spirit of each and every citizen who makes our town open to both new friends and new adventures. Thank you for sharing this adventure with me. I am blessed to have such wonderful friends and family. Most of all, I am grateful to have such a thoughtful husband that makes it his job to keep me on the right path."

The crowd laughed as she expected they would. Donna handed the microphone back to the mayor, who announced the conclusion of the ceremonies. The drum section broke into the state song "The Old North State." It always sounded a bit Scottish to her. There was one thing she knew as she kissed her husband. She never wanted to be anywhere else than right here. There was no one else she wanted to be with. Who needed Hollywood, when she had Legacy and Mark? A few short barks were heard over the murmur of conversation. She couldn't forget Jasper or her family. Maybe she should use her crime-solving skills for television shows, but if a murder happened in *her* town, as a citizen, she would have to help.

THE END

Cakewalk to Murder Recipes

Perfect Scones

These easy scones will have you winning blue ribbons with friends and family. This recipe came from a 1963 cookbook I found at a yard sale.

Ingredients
2 c. flour
4 tsp of baking powder
¼ c. sugar
3 Tbsp. butter
1 ½ c. chopped dates
1 egg, beaten
½ c. milk
cinnamon

Directions

Heat oven to 350. Mix into soft dough. Roll out and cut into 2 x 3-inch triangles ¼ inch thick. Using a pastry brush spread with soft butter and sprinkle with cinnamon. Bake 20 minutes or until golden brown.

Makes 18 scones

Cheesy Garlic Biscuits

These are a favorite at The Croaking Frog restaurant. To cut down on the time, use ready-made biscuit mix.

Ingredients
2 c. Bisquick or other brand biscuit mix
1 c. shredded sharp cheddar cheese
2/3 c. milk
¼ c. butter
¼ tsp. of garlic powder

Directions

Preheat oven to 450 degrees. Grease baking sheet or use pastry sheet paper. Mix biscuit mix, cheese, milk together until soft and doughy. Drop by spoonful onto baking sheet. Bake for eight to ten minute or until lightly browned. Heat butter and garlic powder together in a small sauce pan until butter is melted. Mix well, then brushed onto warm cooked biscuits with a pastry brush. Serve immediately.

Marjorie's Wickedly Good Devil's Food Cake

This recipe supposedly snagged Marjorie a place in the bake-off.

Ingredients

½ cake of Baker's unsweetened chocolate (2 oz.)

1 c. milk

½ c. of sugar

½ c. margarine

1 c. sugar

¾ c. of milk

2 eggs

2 c. of flour (sifted)

1 tsp. of salt

2 tsp. of baking soda

3 Tbsp. of hot water

Directions

Mix together the first three ingredients in a sauce pan using low heat. Stir while heating. When thick, remove from heat and add 2 tsp. of vanilla and allow to cool.

Preheat oven to 350. Cream margarine and sugar together (ingredients 4 & 5), add one egg at a time, mix, then add, milk. Dissolve soda into the hot water, then add to mix. While stirring, gradually add flour, a handful at a time. When mixture is smooth, add in chocolate mixture. Bake in two greased cake pans for 25 minutes. (Nine-inch cake pans are better to prevent it from running over.)

Icing for Cake

Ingredients
2 c. sugar
½ c. water
4 beaten egg whites

Directions

Cook water and sugar until it spins a thin thread. Pour over four beaten egg whites and mix well. Add tsp of vanilla. Food coloring can be added if you prefer a specific color. Mix well again, then spread over cake.

Dog Park Romeo

THE CLOUDS MOVED aside allowing the sun to shine briefly on the icicle-laden buildings and the dirty snow piled up in the parking lot. People bundled up in thick coats hurried to the businesses, all except two women accompanied by a large black dog. They strolled casually to a restaurant while talking.

The first woman glanced up at the sky and shook her head. "Winter lasts forever or it seems to. In Indiana, all you have are cold, gray days that stretch into infinity, especially after the Christmas rush is over. Decorated trees started showing up in stores in October, and the radio stations started playing 'The Little Drummer Boy' before it was even Thanksgiving. Don't get me started on all those holiday romance movies and now *this*."

Her arm stretched out indicating businesses bare of holiday decorations and only sporting a few icicles, which, located right over their door, had the tendency to drip a freezing drop whenever someone entered or exited.

"Karly," Nala prompted, seizing an opening. She knew good and well her best friend was avoiding her earlier question. "Speaking of romance, whatever happened to you and Harry? You two were inseparable after Comic Con."

"Oh, that didn't work out." She sighed a little, then said, "Happiness is a journey, not a destination."

Nala stopped, pulling her dog to a stop as she did so. He sported a harness with an aluminum handle better suited for a blind person. She slipped on a pair of dark glasses to match the image. "Oh please. Everyone who says happiness is a journey is already where they want to be. Sure, it's easy to say it's not about the goal when you're sitting in some big bucks mansion or starring on a hit television show."

"It *could* be about the journey."

"Give me a break." She pushed up the slipping dark glasses. "I hate doing this, but you know in the winter months there's no outside dining, and most restaurants aren't accepting about dogs inside."

"Yeah, what's up with that?" asked the dog in question. Max, the handsome, black shepherd mix could speak, but would not bark on command for some reason. Instead, he could speak in English, courtesy of a disgruntled girlfriend—who happened to be a witch— of his first owner. Despite all the movies and children's books about talking dogs, most people weren't cool about it.

"Not now, Max. We're talking about Harry," Nala reminded both her dog and her best friend.

"Let's just say it was fun while it lasted, but it's over now."

"Really? That's it?" She stumbled as they approached the entrance of the restaurant. "These glasses are too dark. I hope this works"

Karly reached out to cup her friend's elbow when Max spoke. "Leading her is *my* job. You, the one with hands, can open the door."

Instead, a few diners leaving pushed open the door, releasing the smell of barbecued meat and onions, which caused Max to moan. "I expect some quality meat thrown under the table."

The exiting diners murmured among themselves, probably commenting on the deep voice that either she or Karly had. It became apparent—shortly after she rescued Max from the dog shelter where her best friend worked—that people don't believe in talking dogs. She'd just come off sounding crazy if she mentioned the subject. It was probably best not to. Many would take advantage of the situation.

"Step up," Karly instructed. "I'm surprised your guide dog didn't make you aware of the threshold."

The comment made Max surge forward, almost tripping her. She managed to regain her balance and made it into the restaurant where the hostess asked if they wanted a handicapped table. Nala wasn't even sure what that meant. Was the table different somehow? "No, a large booth will do."

They made it to the booth without any mishaps. The waitress hurried off to find the one braille menu they had, giving Max time to settle underneath the table. Nala pulled the glasses down enough to take in the booth before sliding into it. "I'm not sure how anyone sees anything with these glasses on."

Karly laughed and coughed. "Think about it."

"Yeah, I know. As soon as I said it, I realized the obvious. By the way, I want the chicken barbecue sandwich with sweet potato fries. Oh, and an iced tea to drink." Max shoved her leg with his heavy body. "Add a Texas Brisket with no sauce and steak fries."

Her friend chuckled. "Good luck getting him to eat kibble after brisket."

"Tell me about it."

The server showed up with glasses of water. She placed one in front of Nala and told her it was there. Nala had to suppress saying anything since the action was a courtesy for a sight-impaired customer.

Karly remembered to ask for a pan of water for Max.

"Thanks, bestie. Max will be thirsty after wolfing down all the smoked meat. So, tell me what went wrong with Harry. He seemed like a nice guy to me."

"Me, too," Max commented from under the table.

Nala nudged her chatty pet with the toe of her boot but had already learned he often spoke at inappropriate times and refused to speak when she wanted him to—like the time she was trying to convince her mother she didn't have a man hidden in her office after hearing Max's voice on the intercom.

"He *is* a nice guy." A wistful expression conveyed her thoughts on the man. "He's sweet, kind, and well, a doofus. All the things I like in a male."

"What's the issue?" It didn't make sense her friend would throw away a perfectly acceptable man, especially since she'd been on the hunt so long.

"It might just be me," Karly stated. "I don't trust a man who doesn't own a dog or any kind of pet for that matter."

She understood her friend's huge love for dogs. Why else would she work at the shelter when she could make much more money elsewhere? "You don't own a dog."

"I want to, but my apartment won't let me. I've saved Boston, the terrier mix, countless times by falsifying his date of entry. I eventually got him into a breed specific rescue group. That's my go-to when I can't get an animal adopted. You know I love animals. It's hard to love a man who doesn't love them, too."

"I think you're making a snap judgment. Harry keeps dog treats in his office for Max. That's not the action of a dog-hating individual."

From underneath the table, Max added. "He's the man. Good treats, too. None of that cheap stuff that's too salty and hard."

"He never told me about the dog treats." Her fingers went up to rub her temples. "Maybe I was too hasty."

Nala nodded—not that she had room to criticize after her treatment of Officer Tyler Goodnight. The handsome veteran turned cop still made appearances in her daydreams and the occasional night dream. "Did you tell him why you didn't want to see him?"

"Of course not. I was just busy. Eventually, Harry stopped calling as much. It's been at least a couple of weeks since I've heard from him."

"The slow fade. I can't believe it. You were never a fan when it was used on *you*." Even though Nala had never been a big fan of her friend's previous boyfriends, she disliked how they left the scene even more. Usually, they forgot to return texts, phone calls, etc. One even hid behind a locked door when Karly showed up to see if he was okay after he updated his social status to dead.

"That's why I never mentioned it. I knew you would become all fussy and judgy on me."

Before she could bristle at the label, an employee arrived with the food, causing Max to lurch up and hit his head on the table. "Ouch!"

"Oh, did I burn you?" the server asked in horror. "I didn't mean to. That last thing I'd ever want to do is hurt a blind person. I figure you've got enough problems making it through your day to day life. You'll never be able to enjoy a movie in those lounger seats."

Nala held up her hand to stop the ramble. "Please. I'm okay. No worries."

When the server left, she picked up a slice of brisket and moved it under the table where Max gently took it from her fingers.

Karly stirred sweetener into her glass of tea. "I'm glad you stopped the man before he listed everything you couldn't do as a sight-impaired person. You know Jenny, who works at the shelter, is legally blind. She still goes to the movies. She gets these special headphones that tell her what's going on when the characters aren't speaking. So, he's wrong about the movie part."

"I figured as much. I could have left Max behind, but I have a case that might be right up your alley. Remember how you were always begging to help me? Most of the time, I don't have enough work for two people. Since Sawyer started working with me, he helps me out whenever I don't need a specific gender for undercover work."

Karly stuck her tongue out at her, letting her know her feelings about that.

"I could see that. My eyes must be adapting to the glasses. Anyhow, this new case, or I should say *cases,* should be golden, or at least, just right for you." She stopped to take a bite of her sandwich before it got cold. The sweet and tangy barbecue sauce was exactly as she remembered.

Using a fry as a prop, Karly waved it in Nala's direction. "You're going to do that, tell me how something is perfect for me, then stop?"

"Eating," she managed between bites. She took a handful of steak fries and put them beside her on the vinyl seat where Max could take them at his leisure. They vanished immediately. Leisure was never a word Max used with food. As a dog who had been out on the streets, she should expect as much.

Karly popped the fry into her mouth and chewed. She still managed to convey annoyance with lowered brows and a wrinkled nose.

Making her friend wait was mean of her. Brownies! She reverted to one of her cookie curses her father had encouraged her to use when she was caught as a pre-teen using a not so sugary word. The habit had stuck, which made it difficult to convince clients she was a hard-boiled private eye. Sometimes, she enjoyed teasing her friend, who could be a little over dramatic. Not too much or she would be as bad as Elvin, her subcontractor and friend who was never above pulling a practical joke. He was the one who got the harness and service dog vest for Max.

At the time, he had been dog-sitting while Nala and Karly went on a wine tour. His goal was to solicit sympathy from women he assumed would feel sorry for a blind guy. Instead, he was tossed out of the bar by the boyfriend of the woman he'd been flirting with. He later gave the supplies to Nala, thinking she could make better use of them.

The possibility of her acting like Elvin had her swallowing in a hurry to speak. "Okay, I've had two clients come to me about a man they met at the dog park."

Her friend's shoulders went up in a shrug. "Not surprising. Men try to meet women at the dog park all the time. I've even had men come into the shelter and ask me what breed attracts the most babes. I was always leery about letting them adopt. My fellow employees, not as much. Usually, those dogs left on Friday and came back on a Monday because they didn't work the expected magic. No dog can make up for a creepy owner. I imagined those guys were hustlers, offering to walk their dogs or something."

"No." She wiped at a dribble of barbecue sauce before continuing. "Lois, my first client, claimed he was charming—a handsome fellow who called himself Allan. He had a gorgeous golden retriever."

"How is this a problem? I've been to the park a lot with rescue dogs, and I've never had a guy flirt with me."

"You're probably better off. This guy asks for money on the first date and never asks for a second."

"Huh? You mean he's asking women for money at the park? That would be a turn-off for me. What's the deal?"

That was indeed the question. She exhaled audibly. "At this point, I don't know. Lois told me she went out with Allan, and the date went well until the end when the man started crying."

"That has never happened to me, and if it did, I would not throw money at the guy. I'd excuse myself to the restroom and hope he got it back together before I returned after a reasonable length of time. What's the deal?"

Many women wouldn't return to the table, but her tender-hearted friend would. Lois had to be cut from the same cloth. "He told Lois his dog had heartworms and had to undergo the treatment, but he had just lost his job and couldn't afford the thousand dollars. Lois fell for it and gave him the money."

The grimace said more about Karly's feeling about the tale than the tenderloin she was consuming, which Nala knew to be extraordinary, pretty much like everything on the menu. "Yeah, I thought it sounded suspicious, too. Why would you ask someone out when you couldn't even afford your own dog's medical treatment?"

Karly slapped the table. "That's dirty, but at least his dog will get treatment. It's better than those who surrender their dogs to the shelter due to medical expenses. They don't want to hear the low-cost options they could use, either."

Her friend had missed the point, which Nala had been afraid of. "I don't think his dog *had* heartworms. She told me the dog ran everywhere, just like a dog food commercial, with no obvious signs of being winded."

"That *does* sound suspicious. Why didn't she think of that before she gave him the money?"

"He was sobbing in a public restaurant."

"I can see that as being a problem, but later on she must have realized she'd been had."

"That's when she came to me, and she's not the only one."

Max's head settled on her lap as if to question why the food had stopped. Nala surveyed the area but halted when she realized a blind woman wouldn't. She slipped the brisket plate under the table, which kept her dog busy.

"Is Allan trying this on all the dog park ladies? Don't they actually talk when their dogs are playing?" Karly asked.

It would be logical for people to talk, but Nala had stood in plenty of lines, elevators, and even buses were people pretended not to notice the person crammed next to them. "It would be helpful if they did. The next lady, Madeline, described her dog park Romeo as looking like a young Mark Harmon."

"Who?"

"That guy on NCIS."

"The cute Hispanic dude?"

"No, the other one that doesn't talk much."

"He's old."

"She did say a younger version. Besides, none of my clients are young. They're close to my mother's age. Anyhow, he had a French Bulldog with cancer. It was going to cost eight thousand dollars to help poor Bobo."

"Let me guess." Karly made a face. "The woman gave it to him and never heard from him again?"

"She didn't have eight thousand dollars, but she was willing to start the treatment and asked for the name of the animal hospital. Edward, which is the name he used, gave her the name of the animal hospital and their PayPal address."

"That sounds legit."

"Of course, only she could never get in contact with him again. I visited the animal hospital, and they knew nothing about Bobo or his owner. As for the PayPal address, they don't have one. The receptionist joked about them being really old school."

With an obvious follow up to her statement, she waited for her friend to ask about the PayPal address. Instead, Karly placed a hand over her heart. "What type of con artist uses innocent dogs to perpetuate a crime? Let's go get him or possibly *them*. I'm all in."

Author Notes

Cakewalk to Murder is the last book in *The Painted Lady Inn Mysteries*. It is hard saying goodbye to Donna and Mark, especially considering both characters are loosely based on my husband and myself. I like to think I am a tad more polite than Donna. Never fear, you can't keep Donna from sticking her nose where it doesn't belong. I predict she might make cameos in other cozy mysteries.

Two new series will be showing up including a mother daughter catering team called *Catering Chaos*. The series is called that, not the business. I doubt anyone would hire a caterer who had chaos in the business name. As you probably guessed, there will be plenty of yummy recipes. Both mother and daughter are single and attempt to fix each other up with disastrous results.

The second series, which should be out near Christmas is entitled *Midnight Whispers*. It is based on a writer who works at a fortune telling parlor and hears voices. She discovers to her shock that murder victim is talking to her. Is this for real or is it another character from her murder mystery book in progress? You can be the judge.

Max and Nala have a few books left in them in *The Talking Dog Detective Agency* series. Herman and his crew in *The Way Over the Hill Gang* series have a few more mysteries, too.

Come and visit Indianapolis some time. You might be surprised at its several first-class restaurants and venues. I even have an adorable bed and breakfast to recommend too, The Nestle Inn.

Love to see you. In the meantime, stay in touch via my newsletter. Sign up at www.morgankwyatt.com.

Subscribers find out about exclusive freebies, contests, and personal appearances.

If you feel like writing a review, please do.

Reading takes you to your happy place.

MK Scott

www.morgankwyatt.com

www.ingramcontent.com/pod-product-compliance
Lightning Source LLC
Chambersburg PA
CBHW060431180626
46817CB00007B/2758